AN IMAGE
IN A
MIRROR

IJANGOLET S OGWANG

Legend Press Ltd, 51 Gower Street, London, WC1E 6HJ
info@legendtimesgroup.co.uk | www.legendpress.co.uk

Contents © Ijangolet S Ogwang 2018
The right of the above author to be identified as the author of this work has been asserted in accordance with the Copyright, Designs and Patents Act 1988. British Library Cataloguing in Publication Data available.

First published in South Africa in 2018 by Blackbird Books
www.blackbirdbooks.africa

Print ISBN 9781915643728
Ebook ISBN 9781915643735
Set in Times.
Cover design by Gudrun Jobst | www.yotedesign.com

All characters, other than those clearly in the public domain, and place names, other than those well-established such as towns and cities, are fictitious and any resemblance is purely coincidental.

All rights reserved. No part of this publication may be reproduced, stored in or introduced into a retrieval system, or transmitted, in any form, or by any means electronic, mechanical, photocopying, recording or otherwise, without the prior permission of the publisher. Any person who commits any unauthorised act in relation to this publication may be liable to criminal prosecution and civil claims for damages.

Ijangolet S Ogwang was born in Kenya to Ugandan parents, and raised in South Africa, more specifically in a small town in the Eastern Cape called Butterworth. Ogwang currently works as an analyst for an impact investment fund called Edge Growth that focuses on investing in and building small businesses in South Africa. By night she voraciously reads anything and everything. Between this and "adulting" she makes up stories.

This is her debut novel.

To create entire worlds in my mind – God, thank you for this most amazing gift!

This book is dedicated to the girl running towards her dreams with courage in one hand and fear in the other

Mom, my first country, and Dad, the greatest man I have known: you both inspire all that is good in me

AN IMAGE IN A MIRROR

Strange, how humans desire to see themselves in mirror image: staring back from the glass, their parts reversed – but their colours reflected.

Nyakale

The rectangular mirror stands in the corner of my room. It's massive, taller than me, with a rough wooden frame with the paint worn off, like something from history. It was a gift from my friend Aisha for my sixteenth birthday. Carved in the wood are quotes and messages from my friends: the profundity of sixteen-year-olds.

It's my twenty-second birthday. I should be celebrating, but with every year the questions have kept piling up, and this year I struggle to see past them. I used to look at them from a distance, like seeing a deserted house across the street and thinking nothing happens between its walls. Look through the window, though, and everything changes.

I'd hoped my restless questioning would've come to a halt by now. I mean, it's never advisable to knock on the doors of deserted houses. I was hoping that today I would not be so consumed by wondering. But today is not that day. Even power-posing in front of the mirror, both hands on my waist, chin up, shoulders squared, legs apart... here I still am, seeking.

This year I graduated from the University of Cape Town.

If not for Aunty Mercy's testimony at Wednesday prayer meetings and Sunday services, I'd be oblivious to the full magnitude of this achievement. She starts the story differently every time. "It is not by might, nor by power but by my spirit, says the Lord!" – piling on the verses to mask the boastfulness that overcomes her. "Remember, brethren, it takes a village to raise a child. Nyakale is our daughter. Today we have all graduated. Hallelujah!" She offers "our degree" to each of her listeners. "Remember this, our degree, Nyakale. How can I not be proud?"

It makes me laugh, the way her cheeks bunch up as a satisfied smile spreads across her face. That smile has a way of getting into my heart and filling it.

Aunty Mercy and Uncle Opange worry about me, about what Aunty calls my restlessness. She tells me, "Nyakale, see this thing of yours, of wanting to understand the entire world, will finish you, banange! Kale, how can one mind want to contain the whole world in it? My child, we must learn contentment, as we are so blessed. This life we are living here, it is not the norm."

I know she's right, but I also know that we live in a world where everything is relative, nothing absolute.

Aunty Mercy is happy, overwhelmingly happy. The kind of happy that does not need a reason, but instead finds a million. If there is rain, there is a rainbow, clouds do not exist without silver linings and, well, cups are meant to be filled, so there's never a debate about half-empty or half-full. I adore this about her, as I should probably tell her more often. Have you ever known someone who makes the world feel simpler, the calm in their eyes making all complexly knotted things unravel? This is Aunty Mercy. She makes Uncle this way too, because it's impossible to be around a person like that and not be affected by it. It's saved my life.

They are remarkable people, much better than I am. Their love is the kind you hope to be deserving of, one day. There are few things in the world that evoke this feeling, of being undeserving – but not in a piteous way. In a spacious way. A way that you hope to gain room for someday.

This morning Aunty Mercy knocked on my bedroom door; three distinct knocks. Unusual, given she usually knocks and lets herself in simultaneously.

"Come in?"

It didn't take a detective to see that she was nervous. She was holding an envelope, which she quickly placed on the foot of my bed. Her left hand's index finger and thumb rubbed at her right hand, and her eyes darted – she couldn't hold my gaze for longer than a second. I stared at the envelope. Whatever was in it had unravelled one of the most poised women I know.

She told me how proud she was of me. I know she meant it – Aunty Mercy is one of those people who do not waste words. I also knew that the pleasantries were just a prelude.

Then she began, the words slow and rehearsed: "Nyakale, I know you never ask about Inachi." The name she calls my mother, the woman who gave birth to me. "But there's a promise I made to her that I have to fulfil. Here I have a letter that she asked I give to you when you become an adult. It's up to you to read it or not, but it's important that I give it to you." Aunty Mercy paused and met my eyes. "Before you go away," she said quietly.

For a moment, I stepped out of my body, a bystander watching this scene unfold. I could feel my stomach tighten, like my intestines were playing tug-of-war. My palms were baptised in sweat. My mind scattered, a whirlwind of thoughts of everything and nothing. The thing with letters like this is that they summon all your senses.

I have always known of her. Aunty and Uncle were deliberate about telling me about my mother and Achen. Black-and-white pictures of two faces. I would look intently, lost in the image, trying to stretch my imagination there, to be with them. That was at age six, seven, eight, nine and ten.

Eleven was when I began to construct memories. Memories

of her that would dance out of rhythm in my daydreams and when I was asleep.

Thirteen, I grew fond of ambiguity: never being certain of anything made everything possible. I filled my mind with other realities, entire worlds where I could be a living, breathing thing of my own invention. Pain in this world wasn't real – it was a thing whispered about in dark corners by the weak, but never real to me. The sensation was overwhelmed by the limitless places my imagination had to go. I would never hurt enough to feel the emptiness that came with knowing your mother gave you away.

Sixteen. Then I wondered how she chose between Achen and me. If she flipped a coin. We were identical, so we must each have had a fifty-fifty chance.

"Shhhhh, you don't talk about your elders like that, banange!" Aunty Mercy would say – fast, as though her words could collide with mine and stop them escaping my lips. Words that stand like soldiers forming a wall to silence me when I mention her. Her, a stranger. The woman who carried me for nine months.

At seventeen, I wondered why she sent these black-and-white pictures; were they meant to fill my empty memories? Eighteen, the darkness of rebellion shadowed me. I was here, this was my reality, and I no longer wanted to hold onto threads of memories.

Twenty-two, and soon I will find myself staring out of an aeroplane window, with just one question: What the hell am I thinking?

Nyakale. This has always been my name. It lost vowels and consonants and got rearranged into "Kay" by my Grade Three teacher. "Easier to pronounce," she said.

Aunty Mercy's response was to accept. "After all, muwala wange, we are in this country, and ours is not to stand out but to survive."

"Survive" sounds lifeless, inanimate, not like the survive of Aunty Mercy's stories of growing up in Uganda. There, survival was active, done daily. In South Africa, the word had taken on a new meaning. No longer doing, but hiding to make existence easier. Gradually becoming chameleons. I learnt to lurk in the shadows. Drawing just enough attention, not too much. No sudden movements, everything calculated and measured.

The first time I heard the word "immigrant" was not in the house I called home. I heard it carelessly shouted out on the playground by a six-year-old girl. It was this word, not the disdain on her face, that made me stumble backwards, almost losing my footing. I didn't know what it meant, but I knew I wasn't welcome into the fold of friendship that had been formed by the other girls on the playground. I wanted to go home and demand that Aunty Mercy tell me what it meant, but I was scared of this word. Each time I heard it after this, I was filled with the desire to run and hide.

It was round about then that I started to detest my name and the questions it provoked.

Where are you from? What are you?

I am from Johannesburg and I am a human.

But you don't look South African. I meant where are you really from?

And so, the explanation begins: how my roots are buried in Uganda, yes that's where I'm from, maybe.

This name she gave me, complemented by skin that mirrors a night sky void of stars. Skin that belongs in a land closer to the equator.

Being a foreign national means being constantly on trial, or sitting cross-legged across from your identity, negotiating who you are. Multiple-choice questions where all answers are inadequate. I cannot divorce myself from either South Africa or East Africa. It is in South Africa that my various puzzle pieces came together: heart-wrenching moments, lessons hidden in daily commutes to school, virtues engraved on my soul. It's here I learnt to crawl upon grazed knees. Here that I mastered the art of falling at five months – the natural progression to walking at the tender age of nine months. Here I found out that life enjoyed being unpredictable, and that it would sneak up on you when you least expected it. With age, though, I lost the ability to appreciate the beauty of the fall; of learning by falling.

It's here that I heard tales of Steve Biko and the black consciousness movement, of apartheid and liberation. A nation navigating its complexities, learning that black citizens' ability to walk around freely was only one face of freedom. It is here I met Lwazi, the Xhosa boy – no, man (he'd kill me if he knew I called him a boy) – who would storm every wall I'd built, ignoring that not climbing those walls would be the more cautious response for both of us. He opened me up to universes of a people, ideologies, things my mind could not imagine on its own. I loved him. I love him.

With history, this history, I am South African, but not entirely.

I am also not Ugandan enough. I've tried to teach my tongue to pronounce Luganda words, with no luck. Let alone Ateso, which struggles to travel smoothly through my airways. My emphasis misplaced, my instinctive English pronunciation getting in the way.

But, this skin, this forehead that curves from where my eyebrows end to my hairline. The feeling. This feeling of wanting, of missing something that I do not know. Aunty Mercy has raised me on chapati, ugali and matoke; on peanut butter in our spinach and meat. This is how I imagine Uganda tastes. Isn't it silly that I find myself homesick for a place I've never been – how is that even possible?

I see Uganda in the news: headlines of hunger and suffering. I wonder about the people in the pictures. What do their lives look like? I wonder what hunger's favourite colour is, what makes hunger happy. I want to know why suffering does not destroy the people there. If the children with blown, empty bellies really laugh when they play with water. Children who learnt to handle a gun before they knew arithmetic, or those who were never taught arithmetic but still manage to create genius. Which one of these faces of Uganda would I have been?

Nyakale. There's a place where my name does not evoke stares or questions. I imagine it spoken there, in the Eastern corner of Africa. My name celebrated on their tongues. Simple evening rituals, Mama singing me and Achen to rest; I place my hand on her, just to make sure she's there. An image in a mirror.

In the stillness of the night, it can feel like the whole world has stepped off its axis and gone to sleep. The entire day, I've been waiting anxiously for the right moment to open the letter, distractedly drifting from moment to moment. Why had she felt the need to write it? Why does she want me to read it now?

I don't hate her. I don't want to feel anything towards her, and I'm afraid that her words might change that.

I pick up the envelope delicately, wasting time by trying to lift the sticky fold perfectly, without tearing it. I can feel my heart beating in my ears. My hands inexperienced in opening letters of this kind.

Dear Nyakale,

Beautiful girl.
I walked away. A sickness invading my entire body. The following days, my body showed signs of malaria – the light-headedness, the feeling of being hot and then the next minute cold. But the doctors could not find anything wrong with me. The neighbours concluded that the gods had cursed me. I knew it wasn't the gods. This was my body grieving you.

Life. This is why you had to go to Mercy, Kale. I wanted to give you not an empty life, but a life full of things I cannot even imagine. There it would be better; you would be better. Not here.

I wished there was another answer, one that didn't mean saying goodbye to nine months. You in me. We spoke a language, muwala wanga, this language of ours did not need anyone to interpret it. I would rub my stomach, feeling for Achen and you, learning every day new things about the two of you. The first time I held you I felt your heartbeat, unafraid of this new world. Your big eyes opening wide, capturing my heart. Your little fingers in my hand – how tight you held it. I felt my tears come. It was as though you already knew what I had decided.

I wake up every morning and my first prayers are petitions to God – asking that He will let you forgive me for my sins.

I love you. You must know your mother's love is greater than the oceans, rivers and skies that separate us.

Mama

I don't know what to do with these words, written in faded black ink. Are they meant to be the white flag that calls for a ceasefire in the war I've involuntarily fought all these years? A soldier, constantly battling these raging emotions. Wanting to know more, not wanting to know more. Hating, loving. Anger, wonder. Wanted but not wanted.

I sometimes wonder about the war in Uganda, and if I would've been better off there. The danger with war is that one must constantly be observant. It leaves you wounded, and not only physically; the images you see permeate beyond the body and wound one's soul.

I am glad the war is over in Uganda, the war that made her

send me here to South Africa. I wonder if she knows that I too survived a war, one within myself.

Achen

"Achen" means twin, or the eldest of twins. My whole life, it's been a tremendously hard thing to explain why I carry that name.

"But where is the other one?" people ask.

I wonder why Mama even gave me this name, when she knew that Nyakale was meant to go to Aunt Mercy.

Throughout my schooling, the older I became, the more plausible it became to say that my twin had died at birth, or sometimes that she'd drowned when we were younger. On occasion I'd go so far as to include myself in the story as the hero who tried to save her – but the doctors at the Nyako clinic refused to attend to her swiftly, and she died in my arms.

I used to feel guilty about the stories I made up. Over time, the guilt transformed into entitlement: it's my right to tell her out of my life as I desire.

My feelings have always been anger mixed with resentment. I've lived hearing my mother shed tears for Nyakale, her words replaced by weeping and supplication. I wonder if one day Mama will finally free herself from this self-imposed life sentence of anguish. When I was younger, Mama wept rivers often; these days, her tears only visit occasionally.

I wonder if Nyakale knows that she left with a piece of Mama, a piece that will always be lost to me. In the village, you hear things that are not meant for a child's ears. Like someone saying that Aunt Mercy was barren – "Able to accumulate wealth, but not to give birth to a child. What a shame." I often wonder what the real reason was for Nyakale being dispatched to South Africa. If it was really the war and poverty here, or if it was the riches and power that Aunt Mercy held over her older sister – the same way the politicians stand high and mighty, triumphant over those who they're meant to serve. It's troubling, how people here treat the wealthy as more human than the rest of us.

Over the years, Aunt Mercy has come to visit us once or twice, although she's never brought my sister with her. I always hate it when Ugandan-South Africans come to the village, retelling their stories of a Uganda that no longer exists except in their memories. Their children are better because they don't pretend to conjure up this exaggerated interest.

Whenever parcels arrive from South Africa, Mama's "Thank you, ah we thank you!" is too enthusiastic – as if she worries that the simple words are insufficient to communicate the extent of her gratitude. All aimed at guaranteeing that our aunt's "undeserved" goodness does not cease.

Me, I think these parcels are the bare minimum she can do.

The mirror is shattered into pieces on the floor, next to the stool where Mama's hair-oil bottles are arranged, from tallest to shortest. I will tell Mama that I found it lying there. I know that since the mirror is from Nyakale or Aunt Mercy, it is dearer to Mama than most things in this house. In every room of the house lies a symbol of the upbringing of a Nyakale who was never actually here, but who we dare not forget.

This mirror is among the many gifts that have flowed from the Land of Milk and Honey. I was always taken aback by how simple it was – small, round, plain, not even full-length. They certainly could have sent something more desirable. A simple thing for simple people, Aunt Mercy must have thought.

I've tried to find reasons to excuse her for not sending a more remarkable mirror. Perhaps the stories we heard about South Africa, how it's miles ahead of Uganda, were fables, like the ones we'd entertain each other with as kids?

"Mama, what's the matter?" I cautiously pull back the kitenge, already hearing her weeping as I approach from the living area. I ask this question out of habit. I know it's this day that's bittersweet.

"It's nothing, Achen," she says, abruptly wiping her tears and resuming the role expected of her: sweeping on bent knees. Today is our, I mean my, twenty-second birthday. This is one of the hardest days of the year; a time of celebration and sorrow for Mama.

"Did she not choose to send the other one to South Africa?" the village voices murmur. "Then why is she still so downcast?"

"Ah, it's been several years, sister, we must accept that things work out for the best."

"You wipe those tears."

With the years, what's helped is that the gossip and questions have subsided, leaving Mama's mourning to become a private thing, with no jury to declare it invalid.

"I'm sorry, Mama, I wish things were different." We always speak about Nyakale in this cryptic manner.

"I know, my daughter," Mama solemnly responds, rising and busying herself elsewhere.

Every year, Mama insists that we have a birthday meal with the people in the village, to thank God for my life. My friends Cynthia and Sandra are coming to help with the preparations. They're both visiting home: Cynthia's just completed uni in South Africa, and Sandra recently got back from the UK, where she's been studying. I'm feeling nervous for some reason about seeing them later. I'm hoping that in the evening the girls and I will get to go to the village centre and celebrate with some Nile Specials. The centre is where we all gather once the sun has set. We sit on upturned crates as people play draughts and pass around sodas. Televisions blare with different European soccer matches, over arguments about whether Chelsea or Manchester United will win the Champions League.

I love it here, in this place I call home. Memories would never keep me warm in a foreign land. Having been the one who stayed after our O-levels has never bothered me; besides, Mama couldn't afford to send me to Makerere University, let alone out of the country. Most scholarships are reserved for children whose parents are in public service. Had I decided to leave, I would've had an entirely different life – and the lives of the women in the Women's Land Rights Cooperative would have been different too.

But Sandra and Cynthia were always enchanted with the idea of leaving. Thinking only of the good things it could bring, and not the ways leaving would change and harden them if they weren't careful. What people never consider is the fact that the city isn't unendingly spacious, with room for everyone's dreams; from the stories I've heard, sometimes it's the altar upon which dreams are killed.

In any case, I'm excited about the work I've been doing here with the Cooperative – it could really make a meaningful change. We're starting to make ground, but the very people we're asking to amend the customary laws that bar women owning land are the ones who are snatching it, left, right and centre.

I vividly remember the first time I witnessed this, a thing I could not make sense of for the longest time. Aunty Anna, Nafula's mother, being violently dragged out of her marital home by relatives of Papa Oride. The female relatives watching as though it wasn't a problem. I specifically remember the man with a plump round face, a scar under eyes that were too large for his face. He kept on shouting, "No woman can own land that belongs to a tribe she no longer belongs to. My brother is dead, so she must go back home to her people!" A vicious look on his face. The year was 2004; I'd just turned ten.

Aunty Anna attempted to protest, but was evidently overpowered both by the people removing her and by Mama telling her, "Let's just go, Inachi." The two walked arm in arm to our compound, which wasn't too far from Aunty Anna's home. Aunty looking like her feet would collapse under her if not for Mama holding her up. She was weeping, repeatedly shouting, "Oh God!"

I've never been one to question the way things are done in the village. When the women go on their short pilgrimage to the river – that experience houses some of my fondest memories. It's more than a walk; it's an entire learning experience. Or the first time Mama taught me how to mix ugali: once the water's boiling hot, you need to add the millet flour, rapidly mixing it with the water with an even motion. If you don't get it right, you end up with lumps of uncooked millet. I struggled with numerous trials but finally I got it right, and the whole family was excited to be eating food I'd cooked. The satisfaction on their faces marked the day as great.

I remember being five, with a towel on my head, trying to balance a jerry-can of water the way Mama does. I walked as slow as I could, one foot in front of the other, holding my breath – but the jerry-can had no respect for my juvenile efforts and so it fell. One day I, too, would be able to walk gracefully with the jerry-can perfectly sitting on my head, under my spell. I would never have thought that the beauty of being a woman, these gender roles they speak of, would one day become something I detest. It is a beautiful thing, but also a hard thing, to be a woman here. Yes, you can have a voice, but at times you'll be expected to hide that voice in a box and not let it out.

The greatest challenge, if you want to be of value in the village, is to be a girl child. A lot of the elders, especially the men, still look at me and see a little girl with big eyes. Papa Nkura remarks, "A woman's place is tending the pots and not trying to tell us how we ought to farm these fields. This child of yesterday, what does this young girl know that us old people don't know, when she's only been on this earth for what, twenty-two years?"

To which, as expected, I dare not respond. Instead, I humbly bend my head ever so slightly, pressing my lips together lest a disrespectful word escape. Mama would be ashamed and scold me sorely if I said anything. This is primarily why I choose to remain silent. I know it's important to her what the people in the village think of her, that they see I was raised right. Right – I've always wondered what this means, and who defines it.

I used to be envious of Yokolam. The village was more forgiving of him and his pals as they forged their hopes and dreams for our people. The young men sat with the elders, fully engaging in the affairs of the village, sharing opinions on the elections and the absurdities of government officials. Yokolam always enjoyed being important, being called upon by the elders. He truly must have had some hidden grey hairs, for all the wisdom in his head. He was the love of my life, the bravest and most industrious of the boys in this village.

I can't really explain when and what happened, how we got here. We were like two reeds in the Nyaguo Lake, one of the most beautiful lakes in the world, where the waters shimmer in the sunlight, the perfect shade of blue. Not too dark or too light. We grew besides each other, and as time passed our stems slanted towards one another. We were always convinced that ours would be a love story, a story about falling and continuously falling.

But Yokolam was a dreamer; the village was always too small a place for him. This is where we disagreed: he wanted to go away from here and I wanted to stay. How does love live past this? I do not know yet. There are memories we all want to run away from, but he was always more haunted than most. There are days I seek to understand this, and others where I try but can't. I worry that I've lost him to the city. I've seen what the city does to people. It can cause you to hate the very food that you were raised on and made you strong; to roll your eyes at the person who carried you on her back before you could walk. You swiftly learn to look down on those who are, in fact, much taller than you.

In the village, I've grown to see humans as half whole, half forming. It's our choices that inform whether good prevails or evil swallows us. I hold these same ideas about this home of mine, Uganda: surely the presence of evil only acts as a backdrop to the good that must exist.

I learnt this lesson early in life. It's in the sun and how it keeps us warm – but equally, it's in how, when I was eleven, Mama and the whole village prayed to God for rain, as it had not rained for six whole months. The storerooms of vegetables and grains ran low and the cattle were beginning to die. The sun eventually had mercy and gave way to the rain. The village gave sacrifices of thanks and everything was as it should be.

It's in the Nile – the source of water for our livelihoods, but also what consumed Lutalo, Aisu and Samuel whole at the tender age of ten. That day is tattooed in my memory.

We were all crossing the river, the wooden bridge squeaking as we put one tiny foot in front of the other. We paid it no mind. After all, we'd crossed this river too many times to count. We were laughing and lying to each other, as kids do, with the boys behind us telling us how they'd be warriors one day.

Then I heard a crack, followed by screams. It seemed there was no time between the two sounds. I looked behind me and there in the river, holding onto a broken section of the bridge, were Lutalo, Aisu and Samuel. I looked in their eyes and saw terror, nothing that looked like them. Their heads disappeared into the water, reappearing briefly, the planks disintegrating. They fell silent, and we stood helplessly listening to the waters. And then they were gone, and we finally returned to our bodies.

We ran all the way home, but the "big people" said it was

too late – in that season, that river was a killer in minutes. Life is like this: a constant oscillation between good and bad, hope and despair.

Cynthia and Sandra have arrived. I can hear them outside, already arguing about something. Their one commonality was the shared belief that nothing remarkable happens here. Sandra is cynical and generally distrustful of people, whereas Cynthia tends to make room for idealism.

"Change will never come, banange! Just look at these politicians and their disregard for the country, blatant in their corruption as you the people starve. I've been away for three years now but everything is the same as I left it!" Sandra says, snapping the gum in her mouth.

Sandra's family is political, with family members occupying seats in parliament and serving as ambassadors. Her closeness to politics has made her jaded – what she calls "seeing things for what they are".

"It's people like you, Sandra, that are the problem," says Cynthia, "constantly distancing yourselves from the people and giving in to this persistent cynicism."

"Ah, Cynthia, come on, let's be real. Our mothers are still waiting patiently for a change that will never come. This is why we both left in the first place."

One more iteration of a conversation had many times over. A conversation between two people who in different ways desire things to be made right. I silently listen to them, thinking about how after all these years they both have, but also haven't, changed. I have missed them – even this constant bickering.

Just as I think I've dodged a bullet, Cynthia begins, "What I'd like to know from Achen is why she insists on suffering," the last word exaggerated and heavy on her tongue.

This sends Sandra into waves of laughter. The moment would be incomplete without this mockery.

"I've explained myself multiple times, Cynthia. It isn't all bad. There's a lot of injustice to make right here, but it's also home. I really think there's a lot I can change with the Cooperative. If we don't do this work who will save us? No one! The suffering you talk of will persist."

"Ah, Ache, you and these ideas of 'evil prevails when good men are silent'. We've all heard of good men killed without a second thought, just for thinking they can be righteous advocates of progress. Goodness prevailing? It doesn't happen here."

I owe my being to this soil. I remember reading this phrase in a book in secondary school, and it's been engraved in my mind ever since. How do I begin to leave the land that's home to all my memories, when the things I dream of changing are all here?

"Ah, Ache! This is why we've always told you these brains of yours could be put to better use elsewhere. Here, that idealism will soon give way to reality."

I know not to challenge Cynthia, lest we talk ourselves in circles the whole afternoon.

As people begin to gather in the compound, my mind drifts to thoughts of Nyakale. I secretly hoped that today she would perhaps send a sign, a letter, anything – but still nothing. I resent her silence, and those thoughtless gifts – small cards containing money and the words "From Inachi and Nyakale" – which I knew Aunt Mercy had written. And I just couldn't bear looking at that mirror any more.

Hate is a strong word, but it makes my situation more bearable.

BABY BLUE

Blue is the colour that the African sky clothes itself in, when it is calm. It is immeasurable, it cannot be contained. It is the vastness of the sea, and all the droplets of experience that come together to make us ourselves. The Baby Blue years.

Nyakale

They try not to talk about it much, my aunt and uncle. Being separated from the familiar, removed but still attached. Distant observers, listening to tales from home, forced to speculate when there are long silences. Continuing to hope, when the news tells you otherwise. But nonetheless, Uganda is often on their lips: it refuses to be confined to the archives of memory. They live lives of constant negotiation, seeing South Africa through Ugandan eyes, in terms of Ugandan challenges. Neither entirely here nor there, washed up on the shores of a "better life". I still haven't mustered the courage to ask them the questions they don't want to answer.

  The sun rises on the horizon, rays making their way through my large square windows to gently caress my cheeks. The golden and orange splendour reminds me of the round sun with triangular rays that I'd draw in the right-hand corner of all my pre-school "draw-your-weekend" and "draw-your-family" pictures. I imagine these windows are a blank canvas and the sun a clumsy artist. Uncle Opange insists that I start closing the curtain due to a rise in house break-ins in the area. If he saw these open curtains, he'd say, "I don't understand why a child must be convinced to believe her elders."

But I think waking up to the sun on my face and this beautiful view is worth the risk. Aunty Mercy and Uncle believe that much of what I think is impractical, and these schools they're sending me to are educating me to be stubborn, full of new-fangled ideas of the world and its workings.

My aunt and uncle are very conservative, unmovably traditional in their ways. All debate at the dinner table ends in, "Just listen sometimes to your elders without quarrelling, Nyakale," and they gasp in sheer disbelief, eyes widening, at the length of my friends' dresses. "Aaaaaah, Nyakale," they say, shaking their heads, "please never do to us what these ones choose to do to their parents. What a shame!" The lines of difference that exist between us make me giggle.

I understand. I know how their background influences what their eyes see. I hear it in the tales they tell of Uganda – how fondly they share these stories, like honey dripping from their lips! Their memories of simpler days unwrinkle their brows, and in between words softly spoken I hear them sigh; their shoulders falling back gently, like leaves in autumn. With memories, they've built a refuge from the yearning.

Still, I can't help but challenge some of their thoughts, and again, this is not the way a young lady should behave. "Who will marry this daughter of mine, oh God!" Aunty Mercy exclaims at each exchange of opinions. I have to laugh. Marriage? If only Aunty Mercy knew – marriage comes last in line, behind an endless queue of more pressing matters.

We live in a four-bedroomed double-storey home in Sandton. The house is majestic, white walled, with a long winding driveway that stretches from the silver gate to the bamboo-wood door. Inside, it has wooden floors and an earthy colour scheme. Art is scattered on the walls, and a fish tank is built into the wall in the living room, filled with goldfish, and other black fish that I find frightening. Uncle Opange has a study with a wooden bookcase filled with encyclopaedias and history books; this is where my beloved piano also stands. The wine cellar is empty, of course, as in this house we are devout Ugandan Christians, not these "commercial Christians", as Uncle would say.

There's a pool hidden in the lush green forest that we call a backyard. Aunty Mercy insisted on creating a garden of her own in the left-hand corner of the yard. She grows sweet potatoes, sukuma wiki and all the other things that taste like Uganda. Uncle is a partner in his firm, and the house is one of the perks that the company provides. He often exclaims at how needless all the space is, about how he could probably house half his village just in the passages of this place, let alone the rooms. "Eh, this is not a house, it is a museum," he remarks in disbelief. For a man who has laboured tirelessly for all his success, his attitude fascinates me.

"Things are nice to have, but not always necessary, Nyakale" is one of Uncle's favourite sayings. His glasses sitting on the valley of his nose, eyes peering into the distance.

I wonder whether the reason for uncle's indifference to material things is buried somewhere in Uganda, in the upbringing that he and his ten siblings had. It's silly, but I think both my aunt and uncle worry subconsciously that having possessions has changed them, has put even more distance between them and their youth in Uganda.

I remember hearing Uncle laughing jubilantly in his study, a Coke in hand, with his three friends sharing a bottle of Scotch. From the trumpeting laughter, you could tell the whisky had made its way to the places in our brain that house our inhibitions. A night like many when he'd assemble his "Old Boys", opening the closet where he kept his vintage bottles – mostly gifts from the firm that he kept to indulge his guests. Uncle, as usual, sat stately in his chair, with the other three eagerly leaning in. They were all trailblazers in their own right, worried that the more they achieved, the more they needed to remind themselves and others that they were "village boys". Uncle told stories about how, at twelve, his father told him to slaughter the finest goat with no instructions; how he couldn't admit that, although he'd watched this done numerous times, he was afraid. But then he went on to slaughter it with such skill, he was rewarded with the portions usually reserved for guests.

"You know, after the xenophobic attacks, I thought of just packing and leaving. There's nothing like peace of mind, and here I will never have peace of mind."

"My brother, I hear you, but peace also comes from not suffering, and here God has blessed us," one of the other uncles said flatly, like this was an obvious fact being ignored.

"I mean also it hasn't been bad in these suburbs. A relative in the township has shared stories that make one sick. Brothers, we have much to be grateful for."

The laughter died down. "It's this separation, this sense of exemption that scares me," said Uncle seriously. "Perhaps the problem with memory is that it makes you believe that there were no hardships where we came from."

They all reclined in their seats, each one in his own thoughts.

I remember later that night, sitting on the staircase, waiting for Uncle to head upstairs. He sat turning the pages of photo albums and staring at the accolades scattered on his study wall, like they'd lost all prestige. I wonder what that felt like.

My feelings are different. I don't long for memories; instead I have vacant spaces that long to be filled.

We are all seated around the square wooden kitchen table, Aunty and Uncle opposite each other. Starting and ending the day together – this is something we've never neglected.

"At the start of the day and at the end, sitting here reminds us what is truly important in this world of things," Uncle declares proudly before commencing with tales about how hard it was growing up.

"This table set before us, we are just too spoiled," he declares, not looking for a response from anyone. Talking to himself.

Sis Glenda walks into the kitchen. She's lived with us since before I was born.

"Molweni," she says, always jolly.

"Molo Sisi," I respond, and in unison Aunty Mercy and Uncle say, "You are welcome."

My Xhosa is still not great, but I'm more fluent than the parents, who constantly complain about the many clicks in the language.

Sis Glenda joins us for breakfast. Aunty Mercy has already set the table. She does everything, leaving poor Sis Glenda dusting and sweeping a spotless house to keep herself occupied. Sis Glenda has just come back from visiting her kids in Idutywa, a village in the Eastern Cape.

"Glenda, how are the people at home?" Uncle is always good with pleasantries.

"They are doing good sir – Yho! Sorry, Uncle." Sis Glenda still finds it strange that he insists she calls him this.

"And when are you bringing the children to stay here with us?" Aunty Mercy asks expectantly. "They would keep us young, you know."

Sis Glenda just smiles politely. I have noticed that she struggles to accept kindness from us.

Breakfast is filled with news headlines and Uncle shaking his head at how terrible the world is becoming. Aunty always saying, "No, but things aren't that bad, we are blessed." Even after all these years, Sis Glenda seems slightly uneasy, giving one-word answers. She's always been comfortable in less formal spaces, not at the dining table.

"So, tell me about Idutywa, Sisi, every detail. Is everything still the way it was at your last visit? How are the little ones? What did you do?" I start asking all the questions that come to mind as Sis Glenda and I clear the table.

Aunty Mercy is still eating at a snail's pace, as usual, and

Uncle is now planted on the sofa watching the news, with the Daily Dispatch folded besides him. "The newspaper is an extension of his hand," Aunty Mercy and I tease him.

Sis Glenda tells me her news from home as she passes plates from the washing to the rinsing sink. Her face is beaming, like the sun I saw this morning. "Well, mtanam, you know there's no place like home, ne. Because of the winter season it's very cold, ngoku, but also everything is as green as it could be. It was wonderful, everyone in the family had returned, you know how when there are so many relatives, the family is so big that you can't even remember who everyone is. Not to mention the children, eh, they grow and change so fast!"

My mind drifts off for a second, trying to imagine what that would feel like. I want to tell her, "No, I don't know what that's like, being surrounded by generations of family," but I hold those words back and instead ask her to tell me more.

"Well, umcimbi went well ke, filled with laughter and a lot of traditional food, the same mngqusho I make for you. But ey, the people are suffering, man, always just trying to survive." The smile that had been on her face disappears, replaced by one that strains her facial muscles.

Sis Glenda pulls out pictures from her jacket pocket. We look at the them, stopping and pausing at each, in silence. The pictures are beautiful. She lives in a small village surrounded by rolling hills that run ahead, one after the other as far as the eye can see; where the hills collide, deep valleys emerge. I imagine the hills filled with endless memories. In the pictures with her family they all seem happy, if smiles are anything to go by. I clench my eyes and deeply imagine myself tracing my lineage to a small village of my own.

"Nyakale, you are going to be late for school, muwala wanga," Uncle exclaims from the lounge, with eyes still glued to the screen.

"But school is only a short walk away," I protest, my imagination still stuck on a twenty-two-hour bus ride away from here, somewhere in the Eastern Cape.

"Nyakaaaaaaale, eh." Now I know Uncle is getting agitated.

I grab my sling bag, reluctant to leave the places my imagination wants to explore. I drag my body towards the door. "Have a great day everyone," I mutter out of habit.

I remember being younger and walking to school with Sis Glenda, she holding my hand tightly, mine limp in hers. I was a curious child, always trying to escape her grip and chase fascinating things. My mind could not fathom what it all meant, but I wondered why Sisi had to take a taxi and we had two cars. Why Sandton was filled with spacious mansions, but there in the distance was a place called Alex, where there were tin houses in which people lived like sardines. Their families were all bigger than mine. What happened to Sisi's children when she was here, who made sure their shirts were ironed or that they were religiously reciting their multiplication tables before bedtime? I didn't understand it then, but I've since found the words for these paradoxes.

Things haven't changed much. Now on my way to school, I see some of the same nannies and helpers from when I was a kid. The thought that their lives, their years have been filled with the same, ongoing routines grips my heart. Their swollen feet are witness to the miles they've walked. In their eyes, I see exhaustion and resilience cohabit. Waking up at 5 am every morning, catching two taxis to clean homes they will never call their own.

"Morning, Mama." This is what I say as I pass each of these women, a big smile on my face, hoping that the hope in me somehow transfers to them and their day turns out a little better. Wishful thinking, I know.

"Molo mtanam", "Sawubona sisi", "Dumela ngwanaka". These are the responses one hears in a city like Johannesburg, the place of gold and many languages. Each greeting accompanied by a genuine smile and a sense of dreams forgotten. An acceptance that this is the hand dealt, and there's not much one can do but play the cards. Sis Glenda is like family, but the reality is that she too lives neither entirely here nor entirely there. This possibly is the root of her discomfort.

In the distance I see Mama Gloria, one of Sis Glenda's closest friends, also hailing from a small town in the Eastern Cape called Willowvale. One of the most gracious women I know, always asking "How are you?" with genuine concern, not routine habit. Sometimes I find myself literally lost in conversation with her, trying to navigate the idioms she uses to explain herself.

"Molo, Mama Gloria," I say with a smile.

"Oh, Kale Molo wethu, you are just growing so fast, man!" She brushes my face, her eyes wide and hopeful.

"This is what you always say, Mama. So how is Thandi? I hope she's doing well at school. Such a bright spark, Ma, she tutors me when she comes to the house."

Mama Gloria's little girl Thandeka got a scholarship to attend a prestigious all-girls' school around the corner from mine, St Mary's – known as a school of the greats, with many eminent past students. Thandeka is still finding the move from Emadwaleni Secondary challenging.

"Hayi, she is fine, wethu. I keep telling her not to worry about being different," Sis Gloria says.

I look at my watch and realise that I must leave or else I'm really going to be late for class.

"Bye ke nana!" Ma Gloria shouts as I race off.

"I will try see Thandi soon, Ma!" I shout back as I speed-walk down the road.

The rest of the way to school, I'm thinking about Thandi. She often tells me how hard it is to not have the luxuries all the other girls have, how she's ashamed of not going on holidays or having the right phone. Sometimes she tells them fairytales about who she is, creating a fictitious happy ending. Honestly, I get it; I feel it too. Though, if I'm being honest, for me it's cushioned – both by my family's material comforts, and by the English slipping so smoothly off my tongue. I often hear people exclaim in surprise how "articulate" I am.

The other day Thandi told me, "Sis Kale, I stand out like a sore thumb, they say I speak strange. Before, when I was schooling in the township, I had no idea that I've got a 'strange accent' and pronounce words 'wrong'. Then they go on all these fancy family trips, while me, I go to Gogo's for the holiday. When I have to stand up in class and do oral on, like, ballet, there's just a lump in my throat. I struggle with words for all these foreign things. I don't know if I belong here, Kale," she sighed, looking at me with her big watery dark-brown eyes, tears threatening to spill.

I hugged her and tried to comfort her, telling her how great I knew she would be one day, knowing very well that my words provided only a speck of comfort. All her eleven-year-old heart wanted was for the other girls to like her, rather than me, her "older sister" who had to be nice to her.

I get to the school gate and there's Aisha, patiently waiting for me. She's my person – you know, someone like a soulmate, the kind who doesn't require explanations but simply gets all of it. Always in my corner, even when I don't deserve it. Aisha lives just three blocks away from my house, and we're always together.

Half Tanzanian and half Zulu, Aisha's very athletic, with a long, thick afro, cocoa-coloured skin and small brown eyes. I've always teased her about how her eyes get us into trouble – they suggest suspicion and disinterest, when in fact Aisha's quite the opposite: she over-invests with complete strangers, much to my irritation. She's pathetic at small talk, delving rather into deep questions that people usually only ask their closest friends.

Aisha and I are so different, yet so similar. We stand at two extremes: my desire to change the world and her desire to enjoy it. Both immersed in desire. She believes that life is to be lived deliberately, while I live fearful of a life void of significance. Growing up, I always felt the need to prove myself – being the best gave me a kick; but Aisha's always had this disregard for people and their opinions. She's the rationalist, I'm the extremist. This is why we work.

"Duuuuuude, I've been waiting forever! Where have you been, Kale, you know how Mrs Botha doesn't like people being late for her biology class," Aisha says frantically.

"I'm sorry, I just got caught up in my thoughts, and conversation with Ma Gloria."

"You and your thoughts, Kale, I'm sure one day you'll get lost in there," she laughs as we speed-walk to biology, arm in arm.

We walk in and sit in the middle of the class, five minutes before the bell rings. Mrs Botha is already in position at the blackboard with a stern look on her face, chalk in one hand, a duster in the other.

"Morning, class," she says, scanning the room for some enthusiasm.

"Morning, Mrs Botha," we reply in a haphazard chorus.

We are in the part of our syllabus that focuses on photosynthesis. For the life of me, I cannot understand why we study this.

Mrs Botha begins: "So, guys, I know none of you see any value in this, but it's imperative for a well-rounded understanding of biology – the study of life in its entirety."

"Of course it is," replies Cindy, seated in the front row directly in front of Mrs Botha. Cindy's the overly enthusiastic member of the class; in other words, the teacher's pet.

"So lame," accompanied by giggles, is what you hear from the back of the class where the cool kids sit. Lwazi is the ringleader of this bunch, the ultimate jock.

Aisha and I are in no man's land, neutral, with no need to belong fully to any circles that we find childish and annoying. Together, we easily transition from one circle of friends to the next, our preferences as unpredictable as the weather.

Mrs Botha hands out pieces of paper that outline the different aspects of a plant and the process of photosynthesis.

"Grade Tens, I will give you fifteen minutes to fill in all the missing labels," she says, pacing up and down the classroom.

Aisha and I are convinced she secretly wants no one to get anything right, because she enjoys showering wisdom onto our "little immature brains". I glance at Aisha, who looks uninspired by the hand-outs in front of us. I stare out the window and think about Thandi. Mrs Botha glances up, catching me in the midst of thoughts that have nothing to do with this class.

"So, Kay, would you mind coming to the front and being the scribe? You can start by filling in the first three labels." Her "would you mind" means get up and go.

Today, because of my conversation with Thandi, when I hear myself respond to "Kay", I'm reminded that this is not my name but an adaptation for this world. I hesitantly stand up and walk to the board, dragging my feet with each step. I can tell that Mrs Botha is getting irritable. The first few labels are easy, but I can't seem to remember anything beyond the third label.

"I have no idea what number four is," I finally say, timidly, after a few minutes of pretending to think. My voice sounds foreign, even to me.

"You would know if you paid more attention in my class, Kay."

I sit back down. I wonder who decides which subjects matter and which don't, and why I have to sit through this lesson. Why are certain things not considered vital to our learning?

Mrs Botha is now whistling, and gazing across the room like a predator looking for her next meal. I follow her eyes to the back of the class. "Lwazi, you seem to be on vacation in my class. Care to participate?"

"Not entirely, if you want an honest answer." Before the words are even out of Lwazi's mouth, his squad erupts in laughter. Fist-pumps all round.

"You boys, where are your manners?" Mrs Botha exclaims, her voice rising an octave.

These boys are childish, and today this irritates me more than usual. Lwazi is evidently spoilt, the kind of guy who gets by on good looks and being the captain of the rugby team, with no grasp of reality. Cindy approaches the board and silently fills in all the missing labels to Mrs Botha's satisfaction.

Aisha and I walk towards the school gates side by side. The weather is a little nippy, our dark green uniforms blowing gently in the wind under our white jerseys and blazers. Initially, neither of us says anything; it's been a tiring day.

Aisha has been quieter than usual all day; I could tell her mind wasn't here. I'd been biting my tongue, knowing she'd tell me when she was ready.

"Aisha, what's wrong?" I finally blurt out.

She hesitates. "It's my sister, Kale," she says, each word labouring its way out of her mouth. "Her health has taken a turn for the worse." She's squinting, trying not to cry.

"I am so sorry," I whisper, feeling helpless.

I am tired of the things we can't explain, like poverty. Like why Aisha's sister isn't well. We keep walking in silence. Now and then I glance at Aisha, hoping that the look has disappeared; the look of unbearable heaviness.

Aisha's little sister is seven. She's been sickly with a rare disease since she was born, and this is partially what brought her family here from Tanzania – better health services. Aisha's father and mother are both doctors, part of Doctors Without Borders. Now tears are moving down her face. They seem to be falling in slow motion, as though each drop demands she feel it entirely.

"I promise it's going to be okay. We are going to be okay," I say desperately.

"But what if it isn't, Kale?" she chokes. "What if she dies? Only seven years of life, that can't possibly be fair!

And my parents not able to save her. It will kill them. They say a doctor's first patient lost is the worst, but no. If they lose Mbali, a part of them will die with her. Since the complications began, they've questioned whether giving birth to her in Tanzania was the right thing to do. Medically, they both know that wherever she was born, the complications were inevitable. I don't know…" she trails off hopelessly.

I am lost for words. I feel short of breath. Seeing Aisha like this is like a stab at the centre of my chest.

"Whatever happens, we will be okay. You will be okay, and if you're not I will be here with you until you are. I promise." I know these promises are dangerous to make, but it's Aisha.

She smiles a little. We get to the intersection of Fifth Avenue and Century Street. This is where we part. I hug her. I can feel the sadness hanging over her.

"We hope, Aisha, it's what we do," I whisper.

"Yes, we hope, it's what we do," she replies softly and slowly, as though it's taking all the strength within her to utter these words, let alone believe them. She walks off down the road. I stand and watch her until she disappears.

The robot turns amber and I ready myself to cross the street – and there I see this woman begging. Her mouth doesn't move. I wonder if her mouth is tired of pleading, and her body has taken that role. Something makes me turn my face away – but not in the way the drivers turn away when they see her at their car windows, pleading with them with her eyes and her hands. My face is turned away in shame. Slowly arching itself downwards like a flower that can no longer face the sun but instead turns to the ground.

Aunty Mercy's teachings ring in my ears: "Where we come from, we have manners. We respect people. We might be entertaining angels," she says.

Thinking of my Aunty's angels, I turn around, hoping I can call for a retake, like in the movies. Her face has many lines crossing each other, running in all directions. Her gaze is far and steadfast. She wears a long skirt, dusty, black shoes, a beaded bracelet around her ankle and a blouse hanging clumsily on her small frame. My mouth attempts to frame a word, but none escapes it. I look down again, helpless, and walk on, thinking of Aunty and her angels and her God.

The house is quiet, Uncle still at the office. It's a Monday, which means he's most likely coming home late. Aunty Mercy has left sticky notes on the fridge, notifying everyone of the endless errands of the day. I hear Sis Glenda whistling Miriam Makeba's 'Pata Pata'. She's in the laundry room, the smell of clothes freshly washed in Stasoft dancing in the air. I don't want to disturb her – and also, her astonishing intuition will have her asking probing questions about my day. I'm glad I don't have a tutoring session with Thandi today. I walk to Uncle's book-lined study at the other end of the house. My piano stands majestically in the centre of the room, with the white chair pushed in neatly, just touching its peddles. I named it Amani, the Swahili word for peace.

I sit and start playing. Melodies filling the entire room, notes bouncing off the walls. This is what clears my mind. I remember reading once that musicians never retire: "they always have music in them." I love the sound of the keys moving as I play. My music teacher hates it when I look at my hands while playing – but see, to me these keys are dancing; sometimes they tango, but I love it most when they waltz. It's as though melody can travel into our very souls and rock our weary spirits to sleep. Here and now, I am the kind of happy that's so familiar it feels like home. It was at this piano that I first knew I wanted to create something in my life; I still don't know what, but I know I will.

"You just play so beautifully," Sis Glenda says from behind me. "You know, I didn't even hear you coming into the house, Kale."

"Enkosi sisi. I knew you were busy and didn't want to

disturb you," I lie. The truth is, I didn't want her to see my sad eyes and ask me why.

"Kale, you know when I was younger I dreamt about maybe being a great artist, I used to draw, you know."

I giggle. "Wait, Sisi, I would never have guessed you like art!" I'm joking: since I was six, I've watched how meticulously Sis Glenda dusts the paintings in the house, over and over again throughout the day. She stares at these paintings as though she's looking for something she has lost.

"But ke Kale, things like drawing are not things you can tell your mother you want to do. And we were poor. No father, just Mama trying to raise all four of us."

I say nothing, knowing that sometimes there is nothing that can be said. Sis Glenda carries on telling me snippets of hopes misplaced.

"These were different times, ke Kale, before... I mean the only schools we could go to were in the township, and did not offer drawing like these schools of yours and Thandi's. I remember those times like yesterday." Sisi breathes in and closes her eyes, reminiscing.

I start playing again. I sometimes forget how privileged I am. It's in moments like this that I wonder if this is it – the "better life" my mother sent me to South Africa for. If it is, I don't want that realisation to slip away in a moment of teenage moodiness. I want to recognise it. Internalise each emotion, freeze it in my mind so I can go back to it often; and maybe that will be when I make peace with the things I've lost, or traded for other things. Until then, this idea of "better" will govern my life.

I settled with music in high school, but believe me when I tell you I've lived through it all – the ballet classes, painting classes, swimming classes, tennis, hockey, and a whole lot more. I started playing the piano at six and that was the beginning of this love affair. I've learnt that I can do most things I put my mind to, and I can do them pretty well. If Aunty Mercy could hear me, she'd tell me, "A woman never praises herself like that, muwala wange."

I wonder if I'm wrong in looking for that one moment; maybe instead "the better" is this perspective I've gained. Perhaps in Uganda I would have grown up facing barriers; but here I am like a forest, growing unbound.

Achen

Summers are my favourite. Okay, there is no winter here per se, but I enjoy the blazing sun, untamed by changes in the sky. The clouds try to play hide-and-seek with its rays, but I want the sun unhidden, baring its glorious colours and heat.

A ray enters the hut I sleep in with my younger cousins, Kintu and Nafula.

"Wake up, you two!" I must always be their alarm.

Kintu looks at me sternly, covers his head with the bedsheet and clenches its corners. He has no intention of waking.

Nafula protests too. "Ah, Ache, can't you just let us sleep a little longer, what are we waking up at the crack of dawn for?" she mumbles, barely awake.

Mama draws aside the cloth that separates our side of the hut from hers. She has a bright green kitenge wrapped around her, like a caterpillar in a cocoon. "Nafula! But what kind of girl who wants to get married sleeps until noon, you tell me?"

Nafula and I exchange a look, both rolling our eyes. These words are habitually sung to every girl in the village. The upbringing of the girl child closely resembles a marriage-readiness academy, with being wed the goal every girl must continually aspire to.

"How many cows will they give us for this one?"

"If you continue like this we will be stuck with you in this compound forever."

We are still well within our adolescent years, but the inevitability of marriage lurks at every corner. These conversations agitate Nafula a lot more than me – hers is an emotional personality, easily inflamed. I've always felt the need to be measured, to sometimes not say what I mean for Mama's sake; to maintain the peace. Nafula says nothing, harbouring annoyance in her silence.

Kintu is a year younger than Nafula and Nafula a year younger than me. Nafula is not only my cousin; she's also my best friend. The two of us have always anchored each other, sharing a kinship that goes beyond our blood relations. Nafula and Kintu moved here when Aunty Anna – their mother – was forced to come and settle in Mama's compound after Papa Oride's passing. The rumours we overheard said that the two had been married for ten years, when an acute illness descended on Papa Oride. This all happened when we were suckling at our mothers' breasts.

Nafula's skin is dark and smooth. Her eyes sparkle, and she is slender and taller than all of us. Aunt Juliet says she got this from her father. I think she would be one of those people you see in magazines if we lived in the city. She enchants all the boys in the village. Nafula is oblivious of her beauty, though, as if it's not something to behold. She says her skin is far too dark and she'd be better fairer. I fail to understand this. She's always joked about how Kintu got the better deal when it came to skin.

We don't really know what happened to Papa Oride because these are not things that children ask adults. When the elders talk of him, which isn't often, he's spoken about like something ancient from a distant time, far removed from our realities. So Nafula and I make up stories about him when she's downhearted and cannot suppress her longing for a father who is frozen in a time before she existed.

"Wait, maybe Papa Oride is a soldier who got killed fighting for our country," I say, hoping these words will help ease the pain I know she feels.

Her face is still without emotion; this is how I know I need to stretch my imagination a little further and find a better example – something that will get at least a smirk.

"Nafula, what if he travelled in a spaceship and got lost?"

She giggles. "Maybe he's in outer space now, looking down at us and laughing!"

We can make each other laugh until our stomachs hurt. Our laughter a deliberate attempt to push back the sadness.

Kintu just turned fourteen; he is handsome, with skin the colour of oak and eyes the colour of sand. He's very different to the average Iteso boy. His hair does not coil, but instead it too is brown and forms these soft curls on his head. There are stories in the village that he and Nafula do not share the same father. I often hear the aunties speaking in hushed tones: "Ah, but how is a child this brown, everything is brown! And Anna says he is the son of that Iteso man who fathered Nafula? Impossible." Now you hear an uproar of voices and clapping of hands in sheer disbelief that Kintu is Iteso. Then their voices become softer and softer as the details unravel. They fear we will hear these stories that are not meant for the children.

A lot of things are not meant for the children. The three of us pretend to be detectives and we listen attentively to the whispers, trying to piece things together, but we haven't figured out who Kintu's father is yet. I heard one night an elderly woman drunk on ajon saying, "You know what killed Oride? It was knowing that Anna had borne the child of a muzungu." I have not told Nafula and Kintu about this. These are things better left unsaid, and maybe the elders are right, not for children.

Kintu does not talk, just looks and observes us all. He has not said a single word since he was born, and the village has concluded that Aunty Anna's affair with the muzungu is the reason: Kintu is bewitched. I don't know, there's something about him... he is somehow more present than most of us. When Nafula and I ask Aunty Anna why Kintu doesn't speak, she tells us that he's different, that his silences are words and that he speaks the language of spirits.

There are no schools in the village equipped for kids like Kintu. He stays at home, helping with chores, filling empty spaces in the day with building things from scrap materials.

Another carved wooden building added to his collection of things.

I've always felt it was useless to sit in an overcrowded classroom, where between the talking and the heat you're too bothered to concentrate. The windows have no glass in them, but the air outside is stagnant, so, instead of a breeze, heat occupies every vacant space. Since junior school I've found the syllabus too simplistic – and confirmed by my grades at the end of each term. I should've skipped a grade long ago. Each year my teacher petitions Mama to give her consent for this, but Mama sees it as a sign of arrogance, and arrogance does not live in our home.

I've started missing class, but not to rebel; reading just seems like putting my time to better use. Occasionally, Sandra joins me on my escapades as her act of rebellion against a system that she's never bought into. Sandra is more worldly than most of us; her relatives live between the United States and the UK. She's visited them, and every month I accompany her to the centre to fetch parcels filled with the latest clothes, books, magazines, foodstuffs – and bundles of money, of course.

I'm sitting reading the newspaper in my special place: just east of home, where the hills congregate beneath the peak of Nagoya Mountain, criss-crossed with small dusty pathways. I know that if I arrive home before sunset, Mama will be suspicious. The Daily Monitor headline: another corrupt politician has squandered funds meant for the development of hospitals in Eastern Uganda; in the Lifestyle section, a piece introducing a concept called "minimalist decor". It's comical sometimes, seeing the different concerns of the rich and the poor in this Uganda.

My mind keeps wandering to what I saw on my way from home this morning: Dembe's mother being thrown out of the house by Dembe's father's first wife. Her clothes hanging loosely from her tiny frame, barefoot as she flung herself to the ground, repeatedly pleading with the other wife, God, someone, anyone to save her. "What did I do to deserve this!" she shouted, head tilted towards the sky. The thing with land is that it isn't just a matter of a homestead; it's an entire livelihood. The first wife tying Dembe's mother's belongings in a blue kitenge and placing them in red basin. "Woman, get up! There's nothing for you here." Not even a hint of remorse, just righteousness. It's the look of desolation in Dembe's mother's eyes that I can't seem to erase from my memory.

I stand with my eyes closed, arms stretched out, pretending to be a bird, a ritual that has taken me through numerous difficult days.

"Achen!" Yokolam's voice penetrates my wandering mind. I open my eyes. "What's the matter? I missed you in class today," he says.

I sigh. "Yokolam, it's hard being a woman here."

Sometimes, I can't help my jealousy and resentment towards Yokolam, with his male freedom, living unrestrained and unconcerned – especially being his father's first son.

"Come on, Achen, I understand that things aren't always fair, but you must stop this thing of yours of carrying the troubles of the whole world. The weight of it will crush you."

"I just worry that I too will end up normalising things that should not be normal."

I wonder if things will ever change – whether women will ever be seen as full citizens, with a citizen's rights.

He edges closer to me and holds me in his arms, my head like a feather falling on his shoulder, his voice persuasive: "Achen, things will one day change."

This is what I have come to love about him: his steadiness, his sometimes unfounded optimism that better things lie on the horizon. His voice provides a momentary solace, but my mind is still with Dembe's mother, wrapped in the injustice of these practices. I wish that these issues were taught in school, instead of irrelevant pieces of history. I know that this will keep me awake for the next few nights: a vivid image of a hopeless woman being oppressed in the name of tradition.

The first time Yokolam and I met was up here. He was standing with his arms outstretched, shouting things into the air and laughing at the echo of his voice. Amused and entirely taken up in his self-created entertainment.

Then he saw me and came to stand next to me, not saying a word. He closed his eyes and continued what he was doing, soaring in a place far removed from here. I immediately felt a sense of inseparableness – that there would be us and then the rest of the world. I was less alone in every sense.

After a couple of minutes of silence, our imaginations, the sky, the wind, he said, "Hello, I am Yokolam. And you are?"

This was the first time I got to see his features clearly. His face looked so alive. He watched me eagerly, making my stomach tie itself in knots. I just smiled, and then finally got the words out, "Me, I am Achen."

The words seemed insufficient, overshadowed by his vibrant manner. He sparked a deep curiosity in me. We sat on the mountain until it was almost midday, talking about his village, and the stories his Papa told him about the time of Idi Amin – "Apparently the man ate people, eh!"

"Wait, come again?" We both laughed, with my laughter filling in where his stopped. Laughter runs along his tongue – this is one of my fondest things about him.

"Serious, the man ate other people."

I laughed again and remarked, almost ashamed, that I didn't have nearly as much worldly knowledge as he did. I sat wishing he wouldn't stop talking. He told stories so vividly, with so much emotion. It was his innocence and optimism that I loved.

He spoke fondly of his mother, but whenever I asked about his father, he'd only say he was a military man. Never here, always fighting. He said his father was like the wind, the kind that threatens to destroy all things in its path.

"He's an Army Man before he's anything else. That's what it's like, serving this country; the things it asks of you change a man into something else. Achen, I know it sounds strange, but I sometimes wonder if he was a better man before the army. If being the kind of father he is wasn't a conscious choice."

"It doesn't sound silly at all. I do think we're at the mercy of what we experience. Things like that have a way of changing us." I said this because he needed to hear it. A bad habit I'd formed for Mama's sake and now for him, too: truth giving way to comfortable words. We choose who we become – this is what I truly think; but Yokolam wasn't, and isn't, ready to hear this.

The first time I saw the Army Man, Yokolam called him "Sir". We were sitting in his yard, arguing about something. There was a screeching of tyres and a cloud of dust; the car door opened and there was the Army Man. He was as I'd imagined: tall, towering over us.

Yokolam couldn't look his father in the eyes: his gaze wandered aimlessly, like a village dog. The Army Man was big and tall. Stern. His face looked hard. He didn't smile. He walked like he was marching. His eyes darting past us. Shouting instructions. All exaggerated when he was drunk.

"Once an Army Man, always an Army Man," the elders say dismissively. I wish they said more, like how Yokolam's father couldn't blame the army for his shortcomings all the days of his life. I hate how everyone washes their hands of responsibility, whispering like distant observers. This is why injustice will continue here.

I told Yokolam about Papa and how I didn't really know him, how he was lost from my memories. He died when I was six, killed by soldiers, but no matter how deep I travel in my memories, I struggle to find him, even from before they took him away from us. I've searched for these memories, slowly and thoroughly. Nothing.

I often replay my conversations with Yokolam, imagining

us again as birds in the sky, free to fly with the wind behind us, him able to leave all the memories weighing him down.

This mountain is a place of refuge for us, but it also unearths the thoughts you attempt to keep out of mind.

Right now, I can tell that something is troubling Yokolam, his bushy eyebrows arching downwards. "What's the matter, Yokolam?"

As soon as the words are out of my mouth, he gives me his default response: "No, nothing, you do not deserve worry." But the look on his face has already opened the door of worry.

It's almost midday: time to head down to the Kyoga lake to fetch water. "Race you down," he says, and starts running, my hand still in his. I pull my hand out of his grip and laugh as he edges ahead of me. The wind brushing my face calms me. Our legs tumble ahead of us on the steep slope; I hold my skirt so it doesn't blow up. My foot twists and just as I'm about to stumble Yokolam reaches for my arm, steadying me.

I love him for this, his unwavering desire to defend me, but I also long to save him from the shadows that lurk in his eyes.

Mama and all the aunties are congregated around the multi-coloured jerry-cans. Nafula is sitting on the veranda reading something in one of her schoolbooks – an attempt to evade this river trip.

Nafula and I started to accompany Mama to the river from a young age. It's a duty that every woman must grow into: ensuring that there's enough water for life to be sustained. When we were younger, we'd mimic Mama and Aunty Anna carrying jerry-cans on our heads, swaying from side to side as we walked, clapping when the one of us said something that was surprising. We laughed as we struggled to balance the jerry-cans, the little water in them spilling and disappearing into the soil.

"Did you hear about that second wife of John, thrown out of the house just this morning?" one of the aunties begins.

"It's such a terrible thing, what these men allow in their houses, but it isn't for us to judge. We must just be grateful that our situations are as they are."

"Yes, my sister."

Mama always separates herself from contentious situations – although she's always been generous to women in need; like Aunty Anna, many have stayed in our compound. But I wish she'd say something more, instead of maintaining this neutrality of hers. The other aunties would listen to her, they respect her; but maybe it's her neutrality that they admire. The topic quickly changes to politics, then relatives abroad and affairs of the church. Mama is a diligent member of the local Pentecostal church, spurring the other women on in faith.

"Will God not do it?" is her response to their concerns.

In unison they reply, "Amen."

"Let it be so."

The walks are always this eclectic collection of stories and advice shared. This is the tenderness of womanhood I enjoy basking in. We walk the meandering soil path, filled with footsteps of neighbours who'd ventured to the river earlier in the afternoon. Banana trees on either side provide soothing shade and shelter from the glaring heat. Mama and the aunties are speaking and laughing. I love watching Mama when she smiles, her face beaming – when for just a split second, the guilt and longing for Nyakale are gone.

The kitchen is filled with steam and aromas rising from the pots. Aunty Anna, Mama, Nafula and I stand in a semicircle with the big black pots in a triangle in front of us. My cooking skills make Mama immensely proud.

"Ah, but look at this one, only a girl but with the skills of a woman in the kitchen. We will get many cows, many I tell you!" She says this loud enough for everyone to hear that she's raised me well. This statement accompanied by a brief dance, her feet lifting off the ground one after the other and her upper body swaying from right to left.

Nafula and I laugh at her. She couldn't be less bothered by our laughter.

"So how was school, girls?" Mama looks at me.

I stare at Nafula, signalling her to speak. I hate lying to Mama about school. Nafula knows very well why I'm staring, but she just winks at me.

"Just a normal day," I say timidly. Mama seems particularly happy today, but her stare still makes me nervous.

"I'm hearing that you're doing very well at school. Always first in the class! You have your father's brains, Ache! We thank God."

I smile, relieved – and grateful for the overpopulated classrooms.

"Ah, Achen – I congratulate you, now you want to burn all the food!"

"I'm sorry. Mama, you know to get the marks I'm getting, I'm always thinking," I tease. "But also it's not burning."

The atmosphere in the kitchen is jubilant. Aunty Anna says that our happiness makes the food a bit more tender.

"Nafula, you go and bring the bowls in so we can serve everyone, muwala wanga," Aunty Juliet instructs.

"Okay Aunty, I'll be back now," Nafula says, dragging her feet.

She hates this, always smelling of smoke. We're all sweating now, thick droplets dancing on our foreheads and down our faces. The hut we cook in is small with no windows. All the smoke and steam just settles in it. Nafula returns with the plates and we dish up. A total of twenty plates. I forget who some of the children in this compound are, there are so many little ones – and when it's time for food, they multiply.

Nafula and I pass out the plates. We start with the children, as is custom, because the mzees say – them, they have eaten enough in their lifetime, and the children are the ones who still need to do the growing.

Once everyone is done eating, Nafula and I wash the plates in two basins. We sit on one of the mats for comfort.

"So, Ache, will you tell me what the conversation with Yokolam was about today? Please don't leave out any details." Nafula always uses this plate-washing time to ask me a million questions about Yokolam.

"I mean, you know the boy and his charm. We sat on the mountain and did some work, in between his dramatic storytelling. Later we walked to the centre to get some soda. Ha ha, no juicy details for you, Fula!"

Nafula giggles, in her mind filling in the parts of the story she's convinced I'm leaving out.

Mama and the elders, they carry experience in the lines on their faces. They never seem entirely settled. Restlessness brought on by the injustices of war, famine and colonial rulers. Each tribulation stole hope. Even the election in 1962, when we'd finally know what it meant to be independent, to own fully what was always ours, did not bring the life they'd longed for. With the coup in 1971, Idi Amin decided that one man should assume absolute power: he took from his own, 300,000 lives sacrificed at the altar of his all-consuming lust for dominance. These are some of the things that cause Mama to have this distant, wishing, wanting look on her face.

It's ironic that we got our Uganda back from the British colony, yet I still see them here with their NGOs and institutions; here to save us, to aid us. Sometimes I wonder what exactly we need saving from. Yes, with the drought, times can be tough, but do we really need a saviour? See, my problem was always these funny glances, as though we were something never witnessed before, banange!

"Why are they looking at us like that?" Nafula would say, trying to avoid the foreigners' eyes. "Staring is rude, don't they know?"

"I don't know, they just seem to like to stare."

I have a constant need to be able to answer the questions that Nafula and Kintu ask. Kintu asks with his eyes. I can tell he is confused as he stands there watching, half his body hidden behind me.

Our eyes expose the issues of our hearts. Perhaps this is what theirs do too, these foreign aid workers. Their eyes spell out the word P O V E R T Y. That is what we are to them, not people with names, likes and dislikes. We are poverty. There are some benefits to these institutions – but not seeing Mama grovel for the offloads from these trucks here to aid us.

As the evening settles, I'm sitting outside on a wooden stool under the big mango tree. Kintu is with me, drawing something in the sand. Suddenly there is a tightening in my chest and I start to weep bitterly, shocked at this involuntary wave of sadness.

Whenever pictures of Nyakale arrive, Mama exclaims at how we "look like the same person", a mirror image – every time, as though she's realising it anew. Yokolam once told me that we feel the people closest to us, their emotions, and that with twins this connection is even deeper. I wonder if these tears I'm crying might be Nyakale's, and if she's okay.

"Achen, please don't cry, what is the matter?" Nafula says as she pulls up a chair next to me.

"The problem is that I don't know what the matter is, but I somehow feel terribly sad," I say, in between sobs from deep within my chest.

I know she wishes she could do something to stop me crying. We both sit staring into space, knowing we're seeing far beyond the village.

Why would Nyakale have anything that saddens her? Better days, this is what Mama gave Nyakale away for. Something better down there at the southern tip of Africa.

That night, when I walk into the house, I hear someone else's sobs. Mama, Nafula and Kintu sleep in the same hut.

It is not the tears of Nafula I hear, I know this because she is snoring like a wild boar. I move closer towards where Mama rests, behind the hanging kitenge. It is Mama sobbing. I know not to say anything because this happens often.

The first time I heard it, I asked, "Mama what's the matter?"

"Nothing a child should concern herself with."

Sixteen years have passed, but Mama still cries for Nyakale. Aunty says Mama used to have dreams where she'd hear Nyakale crying. I think she wonders if she made the right decision, all those years ago. This is why I understand when she says these are not conversations for children.

I hate the wondering. Sometimes it wells up in me like a volcano, and once I finally erupted and asked Mama a million questions about Nyakale. She let out a sound, "Aaaaaaah," like an animal that has lost its young. She didn't say anything else, and from that day I never expected her to. I've learnt to fall asleep to the sound of weeping; every other night, she soaks herself in tears of regret. The sobs are so familiar: they've been my unconscious lullaby for years now.

I sometimes feel like Nyakale left with a piece of Mama when she went down south, so I would always only live with half of her. Rightfully so.

GREEN

Green is the colour of growth, of transition – of the tree once again starting to clothe itself in leaves, refreshed, after autumn's fall. Green is nature, caught up in undulation, in constant rhythmic movement, in deviation and return and back again as the seasons change.

Nyakale

I'm barely awake when the phone rings. Clumsily, with one eye open, I reach for it under my pillow and toss it against my ear.

"Hello?" My voice is muffled by sleep.

I hear sobs, the kind that sound like they've been uprooted from where our deepest pains reside. Instantly my drowsiness dissipates.

"Aisha, what's wrong?"

"It's Mbali, she's not getting any better, in fact it's worse. I hear her screaming in Mom and Dad's room." Her words are almost inaudible through the sobs; an avalanche of pain. "The pain has taken residence in her body, Kale. It's everywhere." Her voice see-saws between sobs and deep gasps for air. Because pain will suck the air from your lungs.

"What do we do, Aisha, we hope," I say lifelessly, unconvinced by my own words. This is one of those times when words fall short, but you're compelled to say something, just to make a person feel less alone.

"But how? Tell me how we hope, when all signs say there is no more room for hope here. Tell me Nyakale," she says, her voice rising and quivering.

"The truth is, I don't know. I wish I did but I don't. We're in this together, Aisha, you hear me! We'll be okay."

"I know. I'm just exhausted, Nyakale. Mama can't hide her anguish any more; it weighs heavy on her. She isn't eating much lately, and you can see the pain in her eyes. Dad, well, a man is meant to be strong. So he walks around talking logistics and medical terms, like this isn't ripping him apart. Sometimes I stare out the window and he's just sitting in the driveway in his car. I can see he's trembling."

We both go silent. I'm no longer sleepy. Reality has a way of waking you up better than any alarm clock. It's about 2 am, a rainy morning in Johannesburg. I'm listening to the tip-tap of the rain; it sounds like it's tap dancing on the windowsill.

There are never words to remedy pain. Instead of looking for the right thing to say to Aisha, I've learnt over the years to try to distract her instead.

"Aisha, can you believe it's our final year in high school? Soon the entire world will be our oyster." It's a feeble attempt at changing the subject.

"I know – and you can't wait to save the world, right?" She smiles, but her voice sounds weary and distant. "Kale, it can't be saved. There are no normal things left in this world."

I trace the raindrops with my finger as they run down the windowpane. It's strangely calming. After a long silence, Aisha exhales softly.

"Kale, remember in Grade Three, how you'd always chase the boys and threaten them when they teased the girls? You were a feminist before you could even spell the word!"

I smile. "And do you remember when Ms September in Grade Six asked you what you wanted to be when you grew up, and you said you wanted to exist? The funniest part was how she thought you were being difficult. I'm sitting there thinking, this is so typical of you, Aisha."

Our laughter is wistful. Those days were simple. Black and white. Happy or sad. Even when you were sad, it never got on the inside, the way sadness does these days.

It's 3 am on a school night. The maths test tomorrow seems insignificant in this moment, though I know I'll feel differently tomorrow.

Aisha goes silent. After a few minutes, I whisper, "Are you asleep?"

No response. I hang up and try to fall back to sleep.

The sun ushers itself past my curtains, announcing that it's time to wake up. It's one of those mornings where positive self-talk is the only thing that'll get me out of these covers. Who am I kidding – every morning is quite the battle lately.

The air is dry, though it rained last night. I can smell the wet soil as I begrudgingly open my window for some fresh air. I drag myself out of my bedroom, wishing my head would stop pounding. I get downstairs and everyone's already caught in conversation, gathered at the table as is custom, determinedly starting the new day. Aunty Mercy and Uncle sit opposite each other, with Sis Glenda across from my vacant seat.

"Ah, finally, Nyakale! You know, the good book says, 'A little sleep, a little slumber, and poverty will cover you'," says Uncle. "A child who doesn't rise at dawn! You know, in Uganda when I was growing up, we'd wake up and clean the entire house before even thinking of school. Just imagine, it was a fifteen-kilometre walk. We were industrious! Even now, out of habit, I wake up at 5 am without setting an alarm clock."

I don't say anything. I'm a bit irritable – a symptom of not nearly enough shut-eye.

"Leave the child alone," says Aunty, in a feeble attempt

to diffuse my mild annoyance. "These are not our times, and her school is down the road."

"Hayi!" Sis Glenda looks up from her phone in shock. "You won't believe it – last night there was a break-in, just two houses away! The entire family was tied up! I just got a message from my friend who works there. They're all okay, but almost everything was stolen."

"That is terrible. We should visit the family in the week and offer help," Uncle says.

"We must pray when we hear these things," Aunty Mercy says, not directing this at anyone in particular. She does this sometimes, when she talks to everyone yet also to no one.

I'm sitting there and all I can think about is Aisha and Mbali. I'm not shocked, to be honest; this is a narrative I've become accustomed to. But such news still affects Aunty Mercy and Uncle considerably.

"When there's no difference between you and me. What is good for me is good for you. This is when society can truly exist." The words come out of Uncle's mouth like a epiphany, although his face is vaguely distressed.

Maybe he's right, and economic disparities will always keep us worlds apart, with those in the "lesser worlds" always left wanting, peering in.

Uncle speaks fondly about how in his youth in Uganda his days would consist of fishing, then helping clean the neighbour's catch. How then the few loaves and fishes would be shared, somehow always sufficient for the multitude of people gathered in the compound. "This was community. You cannot have that here – we're all too suspicious of one another, scared of things we don't understand. Imagine! We don't even know our neighbours on either side of these high walls. That was unheard of in Uganda."

"Ah, how I miss those days. How I miss home."

This yearning consumes them both. The emotion in Aunty's voice reminds me of my Uber driver last week. A refugee from Burundi. As I settled in the back seat, pulling my seatbelt over my shoulder, he eagerly started a conversation, asking me a multitude of questions. When he asked where I was from, after hesitating for a minute I said Uganda. The muscles on his face relaxed, and he smiled; a strange sense of kinship spurring him on in conversation. He told me about how his mother had died when he was little, and how a week ago he'd found out his father had died.

"I have never cried in my adult life, but that night I cried. What made his passing bitter was I hadn't seen the man in five years, and I couldn't go back for his funeral. Without the right papers, if you leave this country, you can't come back. I have to work here to support my siblings back home. I'm all they have, so I had to stay."

The aircon was off but I felt the temperature in the car drop. We drove in silence for the remainder of the trip.

Although my aunt and uncle are wealthy, and he wasn't, they share this idea: being in South Africa is a necessity, not a choice. They will remain as long as they need to, patiently waiting for the day when it is no longer necessary.

I walk into maths class and everyone's already seated. Except Aisha's not where we normally sit, in the middle. Neutral ground. Since primary school, this has been our ritual. My eyes rapidly scan the room, desperate in their search for her. We're writing our last maths test before preliminary exams. Has something happened to Mbali? I immediately dismiss the thought. No, she can't be... I pray she isn't...

I'm trying my hardest to concentrate on what Mrs O'Brian is saying. She hands out the test. "So, class – as you know, this test will count towards twenty per cent of your final mark. I hope you're well prepared, Matrics."

Murmurs in the class, with the front row evidently enthralled by the prospect of A grades. The currency that separates the elite student from the others. The mavericks at the back of the class steadfast in their indifference.

Where is Aisha? My heart is beating fast, and the fog in my mind seems to have erased any equation or formula.

"Okay, Matrics, you have one hour. You may begin."

Heads drop, and pens frantically attack the white sheets. I turn over the maths paper painfully slowly, hoping that my mind will recall even an insignificant section of the syllabus. My mind is mazes and jigsaw puzzles. Sweat droplets form on my palms. I take a deep breath and close my eyes, then slowly open them again. I still can't recall any of the material I studied.

Okay, don't panic. I inhale and exhale loudly. I'm starting to feel lightheaded, and the figures on my test paper are fidgeting. I look at my watch – thirty minutes left. I close my eyes tightly once more, then open them, place pen to paper and begin, hoping that somehow whatever I'm about to write will make sense.

The rest of the school day is a blur. In body, I move through the hallways and lessons, but I'm not really there. I try calling Aisha a million times, but all my calls go straight to voicemail. Voicemail has never before been so annoying:

"Hi, this is Aisha. So, this probably means I'm busy living my life. Being present in moments, you know. Don't forget to be happy today and leave a message if you must!"

I force a smile. Her voicemail has always made me roll my eyes and smile at the same time.

The walk home alone feels strange. I'm so accustomed to relentlessly debating Aisha on random topics: anything from what happiness means to Beyoncé's new album.

It's nearly evening and cars are congregating in endless rows. There are five young black men at the robots dancing, hoping that their enthusiasm will earn a few coins from the drivers. The drivers are eagerly waiting for the robot to turn green and allow them to escape these human inconveniences.

"Oh, you're so beautiful, come here!" one of the

construction workers shouts from his ladder. Whistles and remarks follow in rehearsed sequence. I grind my teeth and walk even faster, pretending not to hear them shouting at the top of their lungs. There's nothing I detest more than these entitled-eyed compliments being hurled at me. Simmering in their mouths before they're spat out. It gives me some pleasure to see the men's annoyance at my indifference.

I walk in through the front door, my bag still planted on my back. Sis Glenda comes running.

"Kale, Aisha is in your room." She shakes her head. "Kale, this girl came here barely able to walk, smelling just like a whole shebeen."

"Thank you, Sisi – and please don't tell the parents."

Fortunately, Aunty Mercy and Uncle are not home. Upstairs, Aisha is lying passed out on my bed, her body still and lifeless. I cover her with the extra fleece blanket from my cupboard. I open all the windows in my room, trying to lure the smell out. I find the smell of alcohol nauseating. Drinking was never part of our teenage rebellion.

After two hours Aisha wakes up, rubbing her eyes, despondent. Her eyes are bloodshot and her afro flat on the left side.

"Kale, where am I? What am I doing here?" she mumbles, her words clumsily pieced together.

I could lecture her on how irresponsible she's being and how she missed the last maths test of term – but all of this seems inconsequential.

"Is Mbali okay? Are you okay?"

Aisha's eyes simmer, and tears spill. I'm frightened that the wells in her will soon run dry. "She's okay, I guess. I don't know if 'okay' exists in her life actually. She's in hospital again. It's become a routine – every four months, five if we're lucky." Aisha's still crying, but her words are no longer swallowed by her sobs.

Mbali is Aisha's only sibling. I've watched them grow up together and, to be honest, sometimes I envied what they had. Although Mbali was much younger than Aisha, the two of them would sit for hours on end, Aisha attentively listening to Mbali tell her about Grade Four, and her best friend who was a little coloured boy. How her other friends, who were girls, were upset when she said Timmy was her best friend and not them.

Mbali is part of Aisha's wonder; she allows her to relive moments of childhood. And Mbali absolutely adores Aisha – everything Aisha touches is gold in her eyes. I remember asking Mbali what she wanted to be when she grew up. Beaming, she replied, "I want to be Aisha."

They make me wonder about Achen. Maybe one day the two of us will exchange intimate stories about who we are and the things that have made us.

Aisha tells me how some nights, when the pain subsides, Mbali crawls into her bed and holds Aisha's face. They stay like that until the little girl falls asleep. I know that Aisha would take her sister's pain and bear it as her own in a heartbeat if modern medicine made this possible.

Aisha and I go downstairs to the kitchen. I give her two Panado tablets and a bottle of water. By the time Aunty Mercy and Uncle get home, it's almost visiting hours at the hospital.

Only three visitors are allowed in the room at a time. Aisha's mom has relocated her entire life to a hospital ward. She's fast asleep on the visitors' chair when Aisha and I walk in. Her body looks frail and worn down by fatigue.

Mbali is awake, though the pain medication has her slipping in and out of consciousness. We stand beside her bed in silence, each of us fighting the thoughts that a life in balance forces upon you. Aisha holds Mbali's hand tightly and delicately strokes her face.

Her body has been reduced to skin and bones, her eyes not that of a child any more. Instead they're hollow, far beyond her ten years on earth. She struggles to talk because of the strong medication the doctors have her on. There is an idle teardrop in the corner of her eye and dried tear marks tattooed on her face.

I look at her, then at Aisha and back at Aisha's mother. A woman undone by pain, no longer disturbed by how she looks. Aisha is trying to be strong, carrying everyone on her shoulders. I look at her, and I want to tell her to be weak. To feel the things that she needs to. But I don't.

I think back to when we were eight and we found out that Aisha's mother was pregnant – excited is an understatement. I remember when Mbali took her first steps at just ten months. One minute she was sitting surrounded by toys, with Aisha and me trying to get her to stand up, each of us holding one of her hands. She wouldn't even stand, let alone walk. Eventually we gave up – and that's when it happened. We heard giggles and when we looked back, there was Mbali, standing on her two little feet. Walking, admittedly wobbly, but her tiny face elated by this newfound joy. When Aisha's mother and father came home, we couldn't wait to tell them. We rushed to the door, shouting, "She can walk, come see!" – and then in that moment, and for the next week, Mbali refused to walk. She just crawled around in a leisurely way, and everyone thought we'd imagined it or made it up. An entire month later, she walked again, giggling in pleasure.

I look at her now, lying beneath the white sheets, and I struggle to reconcile the memories with the tiny frame in front of me.

"Aisha," Mbali whispers. "I don't know what's happening to me… but something is wrong. I just want to go home… Please take me home." Each word laboured through exhausted lips. "Please," she says again, and the tears reel down her face, but no sound.

Aisha doesn't flinch. She wipes Mbali's tears away and holds her hand even tighter. "I'm here, I love you. I won't let anything happen to you, I promise," Aisha says. I can tell she's trying to hide the tremor in her voice.

The hospital room is filled with premature sorrow. Aisha removes a white facecloth from her bag, squeezes it out under the hot-water tap in the corner, and wipes Mbali's face.

Later, I get home feeling exhausted and head straight upstairs, in no mood to talk to anyone. I get a glass of water and take two pills, to stop the throbbing of both my head and heart. Tonight, more than any other night, the world feels exhaustingly unjust. Why do we form memories only to lose the people that make those memories breathing things? I open the window to allow the piercing wind in; it's comforting to feel something else besides pain running wild on the inside. If anything happens to Mbali it will destroy Aisha.

It's been four weeks, and it seems like Mbali's health is improving. She's back home with her family and Aisha's mom is looking healthier. Believing in God again. It's a Saturday spent bingeing on television series and lazing around at Aisha's house.

"Let me go check on Mbali," Aisha says, getting up.

"Aisha, you went to check on her twenty minutes ago, I am sure she's fine."

But Aisha gets up and goes to the room next door.

And starts to scream. Screams of horror. Screams that signal that things will never be the same again.

The weeks that follow are filled with empty condolences, attempts to say the right thing that come out wrong. People with opinions on how grief should look. Expecting it to be well-mannered, to entertain the guests flocking to the house.

Aisha's mother has started to find solace in bottles – gin some nights, whisky on others. The relatives from Tanzania, her father's family, have moved in and it's a warzone. They constantly have reasons to disapprove of the Zulu wife they didn't want in the first place – and now she's "bringing shame to the family". I wonder if they know what it's like to lose a child you carried.

People congregate to pray every other night, the living room filled with relatives and people from the church. Reverent prayers and songs and cries, no one sure whether these are for Mbali or for the mourners themselves. Aisha is there, in body only, because this is what her father's side of the family expects.

In the following months, I notice how the simple pleasures that used to make Aisha happy no longer do. Melancholy follows at her feet, sweeping up to surround her. I look at my best friend and it feels like she's a stranger. In Grade One, when I met Aisha, she already had a crystallised appreciation of life; an ability to enjoy it as it is. I'm scared she may never be that happy girl again.

We're sitting in Aisha's room. She pulls something out of her pocket. "Wait, what's that?" I ask, my voice revealing my horror.

"Stop being childish." She pulls a lighter from her denim jacket and lights the joint. Her tone is hostile.

She closes her eyes as she takes a drag, exhaling smoke with a passionate sigh, as though it's lifted a weight from her. Then she casually passes me the joint, as though this is what our Friday nights have always been. I hesitantly take the joint. I don't want to smoke, but I know Aisha needs me here. So I try – and begin coughing.

We sit for a while, puffing and passing. I can feel my head getting lighter, and in the end I only pretend to inhale. What am I doing, I think to myself – but Aisha has always been all things to me.

"Mbali dying, Kale, it's like I'm living in a constant fog. Everything's blurry, nothing looks the same. I'm searching for a new normal, Kale, you know?"

"I'm so sorry, Aisha," I say helplessly. We don't talk much

any more. Our conversations usually involve her making this kind of statement and me not knowing what to say.

"So, I've been thinking, Kale, I'm not going to UCT anymore. I'm staying in Joburg – and, wait for it, I've decided to study medicine next year." She stands on one leg and starts laughing, "Life as we know it, dear friend!" She spins around, trying to balance on one leg.

It's one thing for Aisha to decide not to go to UCT – but studying medicine? From the girl who wanted to study philosophy since forever? To "Find the Meaning of Life", as she'd say.

"Wait Aisha, in what world would you want to be a doctor? Stop being ridiculous," I say, laughing. Of course she can't be serious.

"In a world where Mbali dies, Kale, that's the world I want to be a doctor in. I know it sounds stupid but I owe it to her, you know." She closes her eyes, fighting tears.

"But Aisha—" I stop mid-sentence and look away. I loved Mbali like she was my own sister; I want to tell Aisha that Mbali would want her to be happy, to not postpone her life. I want to tell her that perhaps Cape Town, and being away from here, will bring her back to herself. But instead I stand there and gather saliva to swallow my words. As painful as the words are, stuck in my throat, I am convinced they're better left unsaid.

I will hate not having Aisha with me in Cape Town, but I know it's selfish of me to even consider myself in all of this; and perhaps this is what she needs. Maybe it's part of the grieving process. After all, I don't know the depths of a sister's love.

It's almost midnight. The smoke from the joint has found spaces in every corner of Aisha's room; the smell rests there gently. I feel normal again, just slightly off balance; I've lost the ability to tell what Aisha is feeling. Again, we sit in silence. These days, neither of us can find the words, really; we're both just exhausted.

"Kale, let's go to Sam's party," she says this like it's an epiphany.

"Sam?" I'm confused. I've never heard of a Sam; we've never had any real friends apart from each other.

"You ask too many questions! Just get dressed." She hands me one of her black dresses – pretty short, with long lacy sleeves. She puts on her army-green dress and a brown belt.

We quietly slip out the front door. Even if we made noise, Aisha's parents wouldn't hear us. They live far removed from the present most of the day, and at night they seem robotic, just going through the motions. Her mother in a bottle and her father with bottled-up anger.

The Uber's waiting just outside the gate. In the car there's silence, our ever-present companion. I am thinking, who are we, Aisha and me? We were never this kind of girl.

The music at the party is loud and there are crowds of people from school pressed against each other. It's hot and stuffy. The smell of liquor nauseating, everyone intoxicated and inappropriate. I hate crowds. Aisha hugs a boy who I assume is Sam; he grabs her a drink and the two start dancing. I sit on a wooden chair on the balcony, watching Aisha and trying to understand why I'm even here.

Lwazi comes and sits next to me. He's a typical jock. He lives in a universe where rugby is god, like somehow playing for the first team means all the girls should feel privileged to be around him. It's in the way he walks, like he holds the answers to life in all its goodness.

"Hey," he says. I look around, confused. There's no one else in the vicinity, so he must be talking to me.

"Hello," I reply, hoping he'll hear the bald disinterest in my tone.

My voice is drowned out by the music, but the look on his face tells me that he gets it. I'm not interested in pleasantries, or his childish schoolboy sense of entitlement. I get up and walk away, leaving him sitting there, dumbfounded.

Aisha's still drunkenly dancing. "Leave me alone," she screams as I tug at her arm.

I stare into her eyes. My friend is still in there somewhere, hidden behind the irrationality of pain. The summer's gone and now it is winter, and like a tree she stands in front of me, bare, everything lost. Alcohol is meant to make us lose all our cares, but I can see in her eyes that memories are returning to her in waves. All at once, she collapses into my arms.

"Take me home, Kale. Let's just go home."

Outside, we sit on the pavement waiting for the Uber, staring into the distance.

"Aisha, I have no idea how I'm going to be in Cape Town without you. This was meant to be our dream. Together," I say helplessly.

"I know, I know. But Mom and Dad, they need me here. I'm all they have now. Medicine – who would have guessed? I know you think it's absurd – but sometimes we just do what we must. It's the last thing I can do for Mbali, for kids like her, the ones whose bodies are taken hostage by stupid illnesses."

We sit in silence, as the wind harasses us in our tiny dresses. It feels like it's wrapping us in sadness, the sadness of things inevitable, like death and distance. I put my arms around Aisha, wanting to shield her from the wind and everything else. Her eyes glisten as she gently smiles at me.

"I'm here, Aisha. Always."

I close my eyes, imagining that we are birds, and like birds we can just fly away and leave this all behind.

Achen

The sun has set the sky on fire. I am with Yokolam. Nafula has decided to no longer walk with us; "the lovebirds" – her new label for the two of us. The walk to school is uphill the entire way, and somehow one's legs never get used to it.

I remember when we were younger and we walked to school in small gangs with the kids from surrounding villages. We'd stop on the way in search of entertainment, which made the journey feel briefer. By the time we got to school, our uniforms were soiled, as though we'd already lived through an entire day, and not like the day was beckoning.

Oranges have never been as common as mangoes in our region. When we were younger, we'd sit and eat as many as we could, packing our stomachs to capacity, only knowing it was enough when they began to hurt. Once that happened, we'd stretch our pockets and squeeze in one or two more oranges.

"Yokolam, remember this tree, the one that houses magic in its trunk?" I say with a smile, pointing at it. It's a tall tree with many branches, and healthy oranges hanging among the brown and green leaves. The trunk is thick and sturdy. People in the village have always believed that this tree holds healing powers. In the village, you also hear people saying things like, "This one is like this because they have been bewitched" – the term used to explain the things we cannot understand. These days, I'm more believing of these stories than Yokolam is, although he seldom vocalises it.

"You know, people here construct these stories to comfort themselves, searching for hope. It's just a tree, Achen, like all the others, a tree with leaves and not magic," he says.

"Yokolam, every once in a while, it's a beautiful thing for people to want to believe in magic. In something beyond ourselves. You say those words like you too didn't once believe these tales."

"I know – but then you grow up, eh, and realise that some things we create in our minds to make suffering easier. As distractions." His eyes have hardened.

"Ah, you and your cynicism! If this belief makes people's lives easier, isn't that a good enough reason to believe?"

"Maybe it is, Ache. All I know is that I choose to believe in things that are real and tangible. After all, the world is pretty much black and white. It is either one thing or the other."

With the finality of A-levels looming, all that's occupied Yokolam's mind is the idea of greener pastures. His restlessness and desire to leave "this Godforsaken place" are more evident by the day.

"It's just too backward staying in the village, with no ambition to move with the times. I don't mean to sound ungrateful, but it's the truth, Ache."

He goes ahead of me, kicking a small stone. We walk in silence, our breathing heavy from the steepness of the final incline. A group of children on their way to school pass us, excitedly waving. On the other side of the road, I notice another group of children dragging their feet. They have pieces of firewood balanced on their small heads and they're dressed in clothes full of holes. They are talking continuously, with voices colliding as they all speak at once, debating who can carry the most wood. They're fascinated by the children in uniform, but still, within their own little existence, they're filled with wonder; a childish ignorance of the weight of the world. This unawareness I find beautiful.

"Yokolam, look at those children. Do they look sad to you? It's knowledge that draws these lines of difference in the sand. Yes, they should be in school, don't get me wrong – but there's something about their unawareness that's freeing. In Kampala, people are too aware."

He shrugs his shoulders and keeps walking. I think of my words and whether I really believe them, or if they were just a means to win our argument. I turn to catch a last glimpse of the children disappearing in the distance, and my heart sinks. I know those chores shouldn't be theirs to do; just being children should be their only task. I remember the pictures that Sandra showed me of her cousins in the UK: around them, piles and piles of toys and things for children.

My childhood was rising at dawn, walking to the river to fetch water for bathing. Eating sweet potatoes with my morning tea before setting off for school, and when I returned, helping with preparing the evening meal. Weekends would be filled with hoeing the garden and harvesting, tidying the compound and cleaning the fish that Kintu caught. These were things that needed to be done by everyone, so we all remained well nourished and alive. Routines that kept the village a harmonious functioning ecosystem.

Yokolam and I are easily distracted by the simplest of things. Trying to measure the mountains by eyesight, debating how many hectares of sugarcane are in the field. With a knife he carries in his pocket, he cuts sticks of sugarcane and peels them, always giving me the longer piece.

Cynthia's grandmother slowly walks past, looking at us suspiciously.

"My children, how are you?"

"Fine, Jaja," we respond in unison.

"And the parents, how are they faring? Also fine?"

"Yes, Jaja."

Once the pleasantries are done, she narrows her eyes at us: "Why are your hands idle?"

"We were just gaining some strength before we continue on our journey to school," I say politely, a smile of innocence on my face.

The classroom is filled to the brim, the odour of sweat dominant in the air. We shuffle past people seated on chairs, others on desks. At the back there are even more students standing with books rested on each other's backs, trying not to miss any knowledge that Prof is offering. You'd think this discomfort would make people stay away from class, but no.

It helps that Prof, our English teacher, is so well liked. He only recently joined the school, and he's one of the most animated teachers, encouraging the intellectual questioning of all things. He always says that our lips should be as well acquainted with the word "why" as they are with oxygen. We love this – "why" is not a word we get a chance to say much at home, with our parents, so in the classroom it's sometimes overused. He's fully invested in taking our minds on journeys, and we adore this about him.

Yokolam goes to the back to join some of his friends. One of the guys, Oriada, stands and allows me to sit. I look for Betty but she doesn't seem to be in class, which is odd. Betty is a diligent student who never skips a lesson. This is where our friendship began – she'd lend me her notes on the days I skipped class – but her shyness stopped her from becoming friends with my girls, Sandra and Cynthia. They're at the front, closest to the door: the two agree on their intolerance of the classroom stuffiness.

There are few girls in the class. With each new year and new grade, more of them disappear. Always, some girls were absent for a few days each month, when they had their periods; but lately, there's this disturbing trend of families sending girls as young as sixteen away to be married, for land and cows for the family.

Prof starts every lesson with a piece of prose from a writer, and then we move on to debating its interpretations. Today the reading is from Things Fall Apart: "A man who calls his kinsmen to a feast does not do so to save them from starving. They all have food in their own homes. When we gather together in the moonlit village ground it is not because of the moon. Every man can see it in his own compound. We come together because it is good for kinsmen to do so."

It's readings like this that make me more deeply enamoured of the moon and the things it unveils, and not so much the city lights. Prof's voice is light but persuasive, quieting all other thoughts. We listen attentively, perceiving his subtle lessons. We will him to go on and not mind the clock. He reads skilfully, with variations in tone and texture, pausing to see if any of us have questions. Hands shoot up. Out of curiosity, but also to avoid chores like cleaning the toilets after school.

I put up my hand after a couple of the guys have posed questions. My hand's reluctant to be raised, but I ignore it and my beating heart, and ask him a question that's been on all our minds since semester began. When we didn't have an English teacher – and next minute we had one who was what dreams are made of.

I begin cautiously. "Prof, I know this question isn't related to the passage you read, but why did you return to teach here? It would've made a lot more sense if you'd stayed abroad."

"Hmmmmm." He looks around the class thoughtfully. Our anticipation is palpable.

Prof was one of those children of government officials sent to uni in the UK, but who chose to return home. He speaks slowly, to ensure that his accent doesn't make his words run faster than our ears can hear. He doesn't talk about the UK much, except to say that it fell short of his expectations. The boys pester him for stories to feed their overseas fantasies, but his accounts are always brief and vague. It was as beautiful as he'd imagined, he says, with all its royal buildings and clean roads; but with the years, ironically, it began to feel empty.

"Well, we want the things we do not have," he says, his words slow and measured, "but once we've seen them, we remember the things we once had with greater fondness. For a time, you feel part of it – the schooling system, the friends, the excess; but there are whispers, now and again, that remind you that you don't belong. With the years, people begin to change, and you start to miss the steadiness of home, even its inconveniences."

He pauses, sighing and looking over our heads. "In life, we continuously come full circle. There are days when I miss being in the UK. If you remember anything I tell you, remember this: we, like life, are complex; constantly running away or towards something."

The class is quiet, all eyes fixed on Prof.

Just my luck – harvesting season is on the horizon, and Yokolam and I are tasked with hoeing the gardens. Barefoot, mud between our toes, we patiently till the soil, row by row.

Earlier this year, the skies were angry, revolting against us. The drought got so bad that the Catholic priests begged the emurwoni covens to hold a special ceremony to ask their gods to send rain. Every god that's believed in here was called to rescue the people and their cattle – and so they did. The rains arrived and things were as they should be.

The evening sun is warm, soaking up the residue of water on the ground. The combination of the soil and rain releases an aroma of newness. Many bicycles and boda-bodas pass us – women heading home to begin the peeling of potatoes, and men the sipping of waragi.

Yokolam is quiet. I catch a glimpse of the look in his eyes. "What's the matter, Yokolam?"

He straightens up, but doesn't meet my eye. "It happened again last night." His voice is low and angry. "I mean, this time it wasn't too bad. Just a few bruises, nothing broken. See, I hate that I even know what is 'not too bad', like a hand on a woman's body should ever be permitted." He looks away and breathes a sigh, tears gathering in his eyes. "Achen, now the thing is I am a man, not a small, confused boy, but still I hear Mama weeping and screaming like an animal in distress and I can't do anything. I feel paralysed." Now he's wiping away the tears. His eyes like a moon eclipsed.

I wish my heart could find the words to make the anguish on his face vanish. "Yokolam, listen to me. It's not your fault, no one should expect you to deal with this on your own. What bothers me is the people in the village – they know this is happening, but they remain silent bystanders. That's the problem."

He shrugs his shoulders, unconvinced, his face stern. "I hear your words, Achen, I do, but I can't help but feel like I am the Army Man's assistant. Standing, watching, doing nothing. My inaction silently encouraging him to continue. I've thought of..." He pauses, his chest heaving. "I've thought about it in much detail. Killing him. Once and for all. I would use poison mixed in his evening meal – he wouldn't expect it." Tears of anger run down his face. "I worry that Mama will never be free. You know how the women here endure."

I touch his arm gently. "I am so sorry." I'm always offering him apologies, which I'm sure have lost any of the effect they may once have had. But what else can one say?

"Let me know if I can help you with things at home. Anything – you know I can catch fish almost as well as you." This makes him smile, but only half. "Please, whatever it is you need." I say it once more to make sure he understands I mean it. This, too, Yokolam feels guilty for, for needing me emotionally; but this is the very thing I love him for.

"I know. That's why you're the only woman I will pay dowry for," he says, joking; the words feel lighter than anything else he's said this evening.

Yokolam doesn't know how to ask for help, and he's even worse at taking it. I'm still trying to convince him that even if he hates the Army Man, he must take the scholarship that the government gives army children to attend Makerere University. Although his fascination with the city frightens me, the education at Makerere will be good.

I'm fearful that the city will change him, that I won't recognise him upon his return. The city has the ability to make people view all things here as lesser, as inferior to things there. To think that everything "modern" from the city is by default better.

I remember Cynthia telling me about her cousins living abroad. How they can't stand even seconds of being in the village. It's never enough, they're never grateful for anything here; always complaining about the heat, the dust, or how there's nothing to do. The moment they get here, they expect unhappiness – and so they find it, without fail.

I'm sitting on the veranda reading a book. We don't have a television, as Mama believes it's an instrument of the devil. I've become accustomed to reading and to using my imagination, making pictures in my mind. I've managed to gather quite a lot of books – every year, the missionaries who founded many of the local schools donate worn-out school library books to the community; as long as the writing on the pages is visible, I'm not complaining. I'm rereading a book I first read when I was in Form Two; it's like the older I get, the more I appreciate the books I was meant to enjoy as a child.

There are some children in the compound, as always. One of my distant cousins is the mother to eleven children, all a year or two apart, like steps on a staircase. The children are playing, crying, laughing at everything. Mama and the aunties are busy preparing a meal and sharing village stories, aromas of fresh ugali and chicken mixed with ground peanuts made into a paste.

My head is down, eyes and mind entirely immersed in the page in front of me, when I hear a soft voice. The voice sounds shy, not in a nervous way but in a way that suggests that this person isn't used to speaking loudly: "Hello Achen, is that you?"

In front of me stands a young innocent-looking girl, maybe thirteen years old. Her hair is braided into four matutas, untidy from being kept for too long. Her round face is tired, and she looks troubled.

I examine her face, but I can't recall it. "Hello to you, too," I say while my mind is still shuffling through its archives. "How may I help you, my dear? Has someone sent you to fetch something?"

She looks at me silently for a moment, and finally says, "I was told that Yokolam can be found here. I am looking for him."

"Hmmm, he's not here but I can give him a message for you, if you like."

The girl looks discouraged, "No, it's an urgent matter and I need to see him immediately." She rushes through the words, as though each minute she spends here is time wasted. I'm slightly reluctant to tell her who I am and how Yokolam and my life are interwoven. I feel uneasy, and I've learnt that, like animals, we must not ignore our instincts. "Okay let's start here: tell me your name?"

"I'm Sarah. I was told that if I came to this compound, someone here would be able to take me to Yokolam. He's my brother but not from my mother, we share the same father. Things are terrible in the villages in Jinja and I need to ask him for help. I am destitute." Her mouth is like an open tap, words spewing out.

I'm still stuck on her claim to be Yokolam's sister. I know the Army Man married three women, and Yokolam has three step-siblings I've never met. Now that she mentions it, maybe I see a slight resemblance in their eyes. In the empty look they possess when sadness overcomes them.

"Eh, so you are Yokolam's sister," I say, processing the information.

"I am, and I need him to help us, please. Please will you contact him for me?"

We sit on the veranda together, and she tells me about how her two brothers, Robert and Sanyu, have been taken by the rebels, and how recently her mama, the Army Man's old wife, has become deathly ill. "Sanyu sold the land they were meant to plough for my education. He sold it because Mama's medication was more urgent and there was no other way," she says, grief filling her voice.

I just sit and listen, my hand rubbing the centre of her back, hoping to give some comfort.

"Now, they left with the rebels because the rebels gave them some shillings for Mama's medicines; but the shillings are already running out and I will probably never see my brothers again." She starts weeping bitterly.

"Don't cry, Sarah, we will see how we can help you."

My heart bleeds for her brothers, but also for her. The thing with growing up in the villages is that these stories are close to home: you're always only a person or two away from such experiences. The rebels also took a distant cousin of mine,

Jonathan, some years ago. That thing ate his mother alive; she lost her mind from fear of the things happening to her son.

I do not know Robert and Sanyu, but to be taken by the rebels – there are too many such stories. I've heard that when they abduct young men, they begin by leading them to the fields, where they're hidden in the tall rice plants. They're beaten continuously and told not make a sound. This is grotesque to me – how does one remain silent? This is when the boys begin to lose their humanity. It's then that they start to lose themselves, to become something unnatural.

Sarah also tells me that her Mama is not getting better, although she's been religiously taking the medication from the centre. It is possible that the people who sold her the medication defrauded her.

I go inside to relay these stories to Mama. She insists that Sarah stay here for the evening, and we'll see what food we can gather for her to take with her once the sun has risen for the new day.

How do I tell Yokolam? I know that he wants nothing to do with that family. I can understand why he says he hates the Army Man, but I struggle to understand why this hatred is extended to these, his brothers and sister. He has never spoken to them. He is otherwise so reasonable… I wonder if this is one of those stories that turns out to have many more pages than meets the eye.

I try to fall asleep, but nothing comes. Dawn will find me still awake.

WHITE

The colour white is void of substance, and so it allows for the existence of any and all things. It is a blank canvas upon which we can cast our dreams, hoping to create something beautiful. It is new beginnings, a future beckoning from somewhere beyond our present realities. Whispering, "Look, the world is expansive."

Nyakale

Aisha and I are seated in the living room. It's a beautiful day outside, with a gentle breeze. The trees sway gracefully side to side under the spell of the wind, and the sun is beaming. But still, I feel a sick sensation sitting heavily in the pit of my stomach. My mouth is dry and there's this burning sensation in my left eye. My flight departs this afternoon.

In recent weeks, small things have been setting Aunty Mercy off. Last week, doing the dishes, I dropped a plate on the floor and it shattered on the kitchen tiles. "You take things too lightly!' she shouted. "Part of growing up is taking responsibility, which it seems you just do not want to do!"

I was dumbfounded. Why was she so upset? For a mere plate? I mean, she has shelves filled with impassable seas of plates, and still others reserved for visitors. Then, there was the time she screamed at Sis Glenda. She never does that – when she shouts, her voice sounds like it's being forced to do something it just can't. And the time I woke up in the middle of the night and went downstairs to the kitchen, and saw my aunt in the living room. Just sitting there in the dark, motionless. She had something in her hands, but I was too far away to make out what it was.

The mood in the house is sombre as we all watch the invisible dust settle. A whirlwind of things we think but do not say has come between us. Our ankles have grown stronger, from tiptoeing on eggshells. Speaking but saying nothing, our throats strained by words reduced to whispers. Aisha has been living here; sometimes she's with us, sometimes she seems very far away. Sis Glenda moves hurriedly around the house, keeping busy, not holding anyone's gaze – a survival tactic we're all getting used to. Bury and forget.

Now I'm watching Aisha from the corner of my eye. I know she sees me, but she avoids eye contact; the person who said that the eyes are a window to the soul was onto something. There's a lump sitting in my throat, somehow immune to swallowing. I look away just as a tear's about to escape. I grip the cushion in my lap, digging my nails into the cotton, and bite my lower lip, hoping the pain will distract me.

Aisha is looking at the blank television screen, staring intently, like the TV is a genie that can magically explain the past few months. I wonder where her mind goes in moments like this, its exact coordinates; what does it feel like there? She shows me only segments of this dark space inside her, never the entirety. I've seen the doorway, but every time I try to venture through it, she stops me. Some days, if I'm being frank, I find myself thinking those doors might be better left closed. I'm terrified of seeing the parts of her she's buried in the darkness.

It's been five months since Mbali passed away, but time is inadequate to heal the hole in Aisha's heart. It doesn't help that her mother has drowned herself in alcohol, her eyes covered by a mist. It makes it impossible for her to see herself in the mirror that countless people hold in front of her. Aisha's ashamed, her father even more so – because how do you explain having a drunkard for a wife? A woman found at bars, slurring her speech, wandering like a stray dog with fumes of poison following her like a shadow. This is something that marks a family as "That Family" – to be talked about, pitied and committed in prayers.

The death has led her father to bury himself in his work until the early hours of the morning, caffeine in his bloodstream. His eyes behind his glasses are always red. Aisha and I aren't sure whether it's sadness or fatigue, or the two combined. He slogs for hours on end, running a private practice, and then more hours at the hospital. Running, truly. When we're at the house, he seems far removed, his face marred with permanent lines. The kind of lines that only heavy thoughts can form.

This type of grief is alien to us, to our community. Grief that doesn't bring you to your knees, but takes you to other, "idle places", as Aunty Mercy would say.

"I can't believe you're leaving in a few hours." Aisha's finally back in the living room, her mind returned from wherever it goes to find solace.

"I know, it's all a little surreal, right?" I try to put on a brave face, but I know my expression lays every emotion bare for her to witness. I concentrate on a stained area on the wooden floor, fighting the tears.

"Don't worry, Kale, I promise we'll Skype often. It'll be like old times. This is us, inseparable since forever." Her smile isn't convincing, but I know her lips are still relearning this motion.

"Of course! Always!"

We sit in silence, but not the comfortable kind. It's the kind that dries the air. That sharpens our senses and tenses our muscles.

"Nyaaaakaleeeee!... Nyaaaakaleeeeee!" Aunty Mercy's shouting from upstairs, dragging out my name so it sounds like it's echoing, bouncing off the walls. She always calls me like this, repeatedly, as if I can't hear her the first time. She's done this all my life, and she probably always will.

I drag myself up the stairs slowly, like my body's a lifeless thing, secretly hoping to irritate her. When I open the large brown door to the main bedroom, it makes a squeaky sound like the hinges are loose. Aunty Mercy's seated on the white sofa, which is positioned exactly opposite the door, perfectly parallel, not an inch out – she and Uncle are both exquisitely pedantic about such things. The blue and white tones of the room make it feel cold.

I can tell that Aunty Mercy's been crying – like mine, her face has never been discreet. She looks like she's heard the kind of news that makes the hairs on your arms and neck stand up.

"What's wrong? Don't tell me you're still worried – I've told you, I promise to visit every vacation."

She just sits there looking at me, allowing my words to settle.

"Nyakale, please sit here next to me," she finally says, her words like whispers caught up in the wind. Her pupils are dilated. Her frame sways forward and back, forward and back, like she might just topple off the couch. I sit next to her. Her gaze is fixed ahead, as if she's in a trance. When she speaks, her lips move mechanically:

"The first one, I named him Samuel, twenty-fourth of June, 1989."

After a moment's silence, she continues. "He was the most beautiful boy you can imagine. Just like Hannah in the Bible, Kale, your uncle and I had prayed and prayed for a son – and yes, he was 'God had heard us': Samuel, the son of my old age.

"It was June. One of the years where this winter here had decided to be so bitter! The wind was violently blowing, buckets of thick raindrops falling on and off. I woke up to foreign pains, cramps pricking my stomach in different places

– but Samuel was a fighter, always kicking me at the oddest hours; such a strong boy, this Samuel of mine. I looked at the bedside table and the clock read 2:30 am. I got up, put on my gown and bed slippers. Your uncle was not around, somewhere on business. This was before they had named him a partner at the firm.

"I wanted to be certain that Samuel was fine, so I went to see Dr Elliot, a senior of your uncle's when they were at school in Jinja. He started with the sonogram and there was Samuel, so strong and beautiful. I looked at him and I was full on the inside, my spirit was lifted and my heart felt such love. What a miracle, I thought."

She hesitates, her body trembling. I want to reach out and hold her hand, but I can't move. My eyes are beginning to water. It hurts to look at her face.

The robotic words continue: "I cannot find the heartbeat. Just these five words ringing continuously in my ears. I could see him on the sonogram screen. He is alive! I screamed. You just search properly for Samuel's heartbeat! My mind understood, but my body was paralysed. Tears began to form, they pierced my eyes like fire. But in the fire, unlike it was for Shadrack, Meshack and Abednego, there was no fourth Man. Nyakale, my heart was beating so fast I was convinced it would just burst into pieces. The room was spinning and I lay there, feeling so helpless.

"The nurses came into the room and began to sterilise all sorts of instruments, as though it's just another day, another procedure – but this is Samuel, why could they not understand? A nurse grabbed my left hand, slapped it to find a vein and pricked me. This is meant to make the pain go away but goodness, my heart felt wrung like a load of wet laundry. Next I heard the doctor testing the vacuum aspiration before using it to clean my uterus of my son. I heard the sound of life being taken away from Samuel, his tiny bones crushed by this machine. There are still nights that sound seeks me out in dreams."

A silence settles between us. I'm at a loss for words. We are both weeping; I reach out for her hand, squeezing it tightly in mine. She pulls away and places her hands over her eyes, wiping the tears away.

"Your uncle came back after two weeks. By then I had got good at pretending I never knew Samuel."

My head hurts, my eyes sting. I take a deep breath, hoping to somehow make the sadness more bearable. She edges further forward on the sofa, staring straight ahead.

"I didn't say a word to him again until 29 August 1990. Asante, we would name her – thankful, because she would be our redemption, the beauty that is to be found in ashes. But I never let myself be too happy with her; I always left the door slightly open for her to be snatched away. As life would have it, that open door was needed. I fell, working in the garden. I thought it wasn't so bad, but then came the familiar pain. Your uncle rushed me to the doctor, still Dr Elliot. The room I was put in was just the same, everything white in that room, how I imagine heaven. Needle. Anaesthesia. Clean uterus. Back home. The sound of crying. Grief. Not me – your uncle. I was okay. Memories erased. Clothes thrown away. Room, dark room. Asante never existed."

Aunty Mercy is rocking her body back and forth. Her arms are crossed in front of her as if she is holding a baby, gently rocking it to sleep.

Beside her, my heart beats, like it's in hot pursuit of something that keeps accelerating, getting further and further away. I literally feel out of breath, unable to speak.

I edge my hand towards her, then ease my arm around her shoulder, until I'm holding her in my arms, the two of us rocking gently. Aunty Mercy's body feels cold, and deep inside me, my heart is aching.

I've never felt a lack of love. If anything, Aunty Mercy has always been far more patient than I deserve. Watching my recitals, sitting me down and teaching me goodness. I've seen in her the epitome of a mother's love; the kind of love that is always giving and does not know how to ask.

"I love you so much," I finally say.

She tries to respond, but her entire body seems too weak. She exhales and sinks deeper into my embrace. She doesn't have to say anything, anyway, because I know.

When I was growing up, Aunty Mercy would say, whenever the opportunity arose, "Nyakale, you know no things are ever by chance." Now I know what she really meant. I finally understand the sense of loss filling the house, now that I am leaving it.

Outside, all you can see are clouds against the backdrop of the clear blue sky; they look edible. The plane is full of jubilant millennials on their way to university, and parents consumed with concern – maybe haunted by thoughts of the things that filled their varsity days. Aunty Mercy is seated next to me, Uncle on the other side of her. He has his arm around her, telling her not to cry. I don't like seeing Aunty Mercy like this, entirely undone. It helps that I have the window seat; I turn my body, leaning away. I quickly wipe my eyes as a tear of my own escapes.

The hours pass quickly. I'm halfway through Americanah by Chimamanda Ngozi Adichie, a fitting novel for the new adventure that beckons, and I'm entirely devoted to these characters' lives. Then abruptly the pilot's mechanical voice brings me back from Princeton and conversations between members of the African Students Association: "The temperature is a sunny twenty-eight degrees in Cape Town today, with a blustery southeastern wind. Have a pleasant stay in the Mother City."

My annoyance aggravated by everyone standing too hurriedly and then aimlessly filling the aisle, we eventually make it out. There's a cab waiting outside to take us to the residence I was assigned. Uncle insists on planning all things extensively ahead of time. This is where he and I differ.

I'll be living in Graça Machel Hall, one of the newer residences on lower campus. All this is still in my imagination; I don't really know what to expect. I'm seated at the back with Aunty Mercy, with Uncle in front beside the cab driver. They know each other quite well: Uncle, a firm believer in the saying, "If it ain't broke, don't fix it," uses the same driver whenever he's in town on business. I glance at Aunty Mercy, and I'm relieved to see her looking more relaxed. The vein that protrudes on the right side of her face when she's stressed has vanished, and her eyes are again tinted with joy.

The colossal mountain, clothed in clouds, looks like a picture on a postcard. The university can be seen from miles away. The buildings are like great statues, standing in defiance against the mountain backdrop. Aunty Mercy and Uncle are mostly silent, with just a few remarks about the weather, or how they can't believe that their baby has grown up so suddenly.

I've been to Cape Town countless times, on holiday and for school events, but this time feels like nothing before. My senses are heightened, the taste of a whole new life on the tip of my tongue. If I'm being honest, I'm slightly nervous about the mysteries that wait for me – about new friends, and not having Aisha here with me. Especially because the past couple of months have taught me that life will sometimes deviate completely from the script.

The queues at Graça twist and turn endlessly. All us girls line up with our parents, waiting for seniors to instruct us how to sign in and tell us which rooms we've been assigned. The dining hall is filled with scents of freedom, independence and uncertainty. Around me, parents are asking their daughters if they've remembered to pack essentials; while the girls are celebrating, finally relinquishing the chains of curfews and chores. Everyone's impatient. The parents have tired feet from travelling miles to bring their daughters here. We eventually get to the front of the line.

"Ah, it's about time!" Uncle exclaims to no one in particular. He's picked up this habit from Aunty Mercy.

"But we are here now, my husband," Aunty Mercy replies, always the diplomat, stroking Uncle's arm.

I smile at the two of them, imagining them together at the house without me, marvelling at the beauty of old friendship. How all motions are so natural, how Aunty Mercy's arm locates Uncle's with the utmost ease, as though they are extensions of each other.

The girl sitting at the registration desk is wearing a pink V-neck T-shirt with "First Ladies" written on it. "Hello, my name is Naledi – and you are?" Her face is painted with warm enthusiasm.

"Hi, I'm Nyakale Namuyangu." I know my enthusiasm can't compare to hers. I'm excited, but I'm also an over-thinker; my mind's here, but it's also simultaneously mapping out all possible scenarios for the next couple of years.

"Okay Nyakale, let's see." She pages through a stack of papers, listing innumerable names. "So, you'll be on the third floor, room 309 – here's your key, internet cable and security light," she says a little hurriedly, glancing at the line behind me. "Please sign next to your name."

"Thank you!"

I gather my new belongings and head towards the lift, Uncle and Aunty Mercy following with the bags. The elevator's taking forever because of all the luggage, and people getting off on every floor. "Let's just take the stairs," Uncle finally says. "Waiting for a lift, like we don't have the strength to walk!"

Aunty Mercy and I let him grab most of the bags. You can see they're pulling his shoulders down – they're almost pointed at the floor – but it's futile arguing with Uncle when it comes to things like this. We follow him up the stairs to my room, now my new home.

There are two beds separated by a room divider, grey cupboards on either side, and a deep blue carpet. The windows face the walkway to upper campus and a green lawn, scattered trees and cars.

"Heeeelllo, my name is Ntombi, your a-mazing roommate!" The tall girl approaching me is all confidence. Her hair is long and straight, and you can tell it's hers by the thick roots.

"Hi, I'm Nyakale, but I guess they told you that downstairs." We both let out a brief giggle, the kind aimed at easing initial awkwardness.

Meanwhile, Aunty Mercy, Uncle and the woman I assume is Ntombi's mother are exchanging pleasantries, and, from the sound of it, finding solace in trading stories about how lost our generation is. The mother seems astonishingly young. Ntombi notices me staring, so I quickly look away and fidget with my bags; but she comes up to me with an amused smile and whispers, "Noooo, she's not my mother, she's my father's assistant. She came down with me from Durban to help me settle in – and to ease my dad's conscience." She rolls her eyes, and I have to giggle.

There's something liberating about this girl. There's an aura about her – daring, careless, with a hint of wild – and I am mesmerised.

Achen

"Eh, god must help us!" one of the aunties shouts to the heavens as she bathes her baby in a blue basin just outside the hut with a bar of green soap. Her face is distorted with distress. I wonder, but know not to ask, what has compelled her to cry. The woman next to her puts an arm around her in comfort.

Breakfast is being prepared; the air is decorated with the aromas of readiness for the day ahead. I hear Mama's voice bulldozing through the house, again. I know almost certainly that it's because a chore has been left undone by Nafula. Mama's reaction after all these years is still sheer disbelief. I hear Nafula grumbling, but her words are no competition for Mama's, in either loudness or roughness.

Kintu is sitting on a wooden stool under one of the trees in the centre of the compound, having his morning tea and overcooked cassava. He looks up just as the storm begins to rampage inside the house, and smiles at me knowingly. Aunty Juliet never gets involved because Mama's the oldest. Mama's always complaining to us kids, "As old as you are, Aunty Juliet continues to baby you, and that's why you stay childish." When the morning begins like this, we must ensure no one leaves a chore undone; we all tiptoe around Mama for the rest of the day.

But I'm prepared to take it. Anything is better than Mama's worst days – when her uterus remembers that on 21 September 1994, she did not give birth to just one child, but rather two of us. Those days are the worst, the days she longs for Nyakale. It's in the way she walks around aimlessly, searching for nothing in particular, like she's lost her sanity. She walks in one direction – "Ah!" – an exclamation leaves her mouth and then she turns around and walks in the opposite direction. Agitated, still looking for memories to preserve. Wrinkles stain her forehead, eyes confused, and she seems pale and weak. Over the years, I've learnt better than anyone how to tell when it's one of those days.

"Mama, are you okay?" I'd ask.

No answer, most times; but one day, she did respond, and since then I've known not to ask such violent questions.

"I have not heard the voice of your sister since the day she left, just a baby crying. That's the only memory I have of her voice – and that cry, it haunts me. Did I give her to Mercy because I thought I wouldn't manage with the two of you? But have you not turned out fine? Or maybe I just felt pity for Mercy and her dry womb." She speaks the last words with venom on her tongue.

"Sorry, Mama. I'm sure you did the best you knew to do then." I can tell that my attempts to give her some peace fall short.

Aunt Mercy and Mama are just two years apart in age. Aunty Juliet tells me that growing up, the three were inseparable. Now Aunt Mercy is only mentioned when Mama mentions Nyakale, and the two have not spoken in some time. The things that years can do.

I've never quite understood Mama's emotions. Does she resent the fact that Aunt Mercy is the only mother Nyakale knows? Is that the essence of it?

Aunt Mercy sends parcels of money for us from South Africa, and pictures of Nyakale from time to time. In the beginning years, the pictures were plenty and the notes scarce. These days the notes are in abundance and the pictures lacking.

Each time a parcel ticket arrives for Mama, she sends me to fetch it from the village centre. I can tell she feels ashamed when she unwraps it and sees the money, but even more ashamed when she sees the picture of Nyakale and how much she's grown since the last time. She stares at the photo for so long, with such intensity – like she's making sure that she doesn't forget a single detail. She touches the picture, tracing Nyakale's image, hoping to feel her.

It's strange for me to see my sister. She looks just like me – but nothing like me. We both have natural hair, but mine is short. Her afro is twisted into soft shiny swirls. She seems taller than me. At least she looks happy, I think to myself.

The days have started to feel shorter. Lately, I'm almost sure that the sun has decided to set earlier, and the nights are dragging on like they have nowhere else to be. I know I encouraged him to go, but with each day that passes I feel my heart sinking a little lower. It's mostly the fear that one day, when he returns on vacation, I won't recognise who Yokolam has become. I feel foolish thinking this, but the city has been known to make people roll their eyes, pinch their noses, and cleanse their hands when they come back to the village. I also think that maybe, there in the city, he'll meet one of those city girls who look like models, with long hair and a body that gets you into magazines. That's what is beautiful there, not a girl like me.

We've all lost people to the city – even the elders, in their own way. This city virus is a silent killer. It is slow and subtle in its devouring of a person. It will start when you call and get voicemail instead of the person you're looking for; then, when the person does answer the phone, their words sound slippery, like it's difficult to speak, or rather they just don't want to. Then they stop visiting the village to be with the people. Instead they come only to bring parcels; to "help" us.

It's been some time since Sarah, who claims to be Yokolam's sister, appeared on our doorstep, looking for him. When I told him about it, he listened, but didn't say much in response. Whenever I bring it up, he shrugs it off; says he doesn't want to talk about it, or that it's "not something to concern yourself about".

Lately, I've found myself yearning for the days when life was less complex. When we were just children under the scorching sun, getting scolded by the elders, discovering the rivers past the boundaries that the elders had forbidden us to cross. Didn't they know this would just spark our curiosity? When we'd taunt the missionaries by throwing stones at their windows at night – their compounds enclosed by wire, while our huts were out in the open. We wondered what scared them so, to make them build those walls.

Although I suppose Uganda hasn't changed much since then: the same president since the day I was born, people in Kampala still protesting about service delivery. Opportunities, still, for those who know the right names or are born into the right families. "Banange, things will never change," the people say. They've started to lose their grip on hope.

"But what do you expect?" says one mzee – the Elder, as the

old man is known. "We must live our lives the best we can, and provide for our families. How can you place your lives in the hands of a man-made government? What do you expect from mere mortals, if not greed?" The Elder sits with a pen and a dusty little brown notebook firmly gripped in his hands, scribbling random notes. When we were younger, we wanted to steal it. The children would sit around him and listen to his stories about all things: the sun, the moon, the wars of times past. He didn't leave out details like the other elders did. He laid it all bare.

The Elder is always sitting under the mango tree at one end of the compound, or up in the small hills that rise and fall beyond the other side of the settlement. He's very old, his hair seasoned with grey, and he walks with a stick; but still, he seems strong. He's always in a suit, tattered from wear. Somehow, he manages to look respectable, even with the holes in his hat. There are stories about him, as with most things. This old man's lived in the village since Mama was just a young girl; he's apparently more than a hundred years old. He's a spiritual healer, this is why he's still so strong – that book of his is filled with rituals that he performs at his shrine, they say.

I meet Yokolam at the centre. It's filling up as the afternoon wears on: people drinking Nile Specials, their spirits rising with every sip – you can tell by the jubilant voices roaring. Boys running, making the dust rise as they drive their wire cars up and down. The frying of mandazi in oil, splash marks on the women's kitenges as they sit on their stools, pots between their knees. Aunties laughing at the latest gossip making its rounds; boda-bodas recklessly transporting people from the town where they've spent the day trading, back to the village. Women with babies on their backs and wood on their heads, necks of steel. Big kaveras filled with goods from their morning trade. A day's work done as sweat collects on faces.

Yokolam and I are sitting on bottle crates outside the Plaza, with two sodas on the little wooden table between us. It's not a comfortable silence but an anxious one, with each of us waiting for the other to fill it. We're both staring into the street, avoiding each other's eyes: things we've seen for years seem suddenly much more interesting. It's now just one day until he must leave for the city – we've been counting down. I'm excited for him. The other day, Nafula asked if I was upset that it was him going and not me, but she couldn't be more wrong. This is Yokolam, and there's no one for whom I could want this more. Besides, if he stays for me, I worry that he'll never truly be happy, and that one day he'll grow to resent me.

"Achen, I promise to call as much as I can," he says, slicing the silence in half. "And Kampala isn't too far, you'll be able to come see me. I'll send you money from my stipend, you can use it to visit and for upkeep." They're words he's said a thousand times before.

"I know. I know, Yokolam. But I think it's important to accept that things will be different now." I avoid looking at him because if I do, I may just cry.

"We are always evolving and changing as people, Achen. Just think back to when we were younger. We have changed, but if our core stays the same, we'll always be fine. And you know me," he smiles, "I'll always be the boy who loves the mountain and pretends to be a bird."

I'm annoyed – by how he simplifies things; by his certainty.

He continues, "You know I still want you to come to the city with me. You could study for a certificate or find a job – maybe with some organisation that could help you with this newfound activism. The village will always be too small for you!"

There it is again: Yokolam knows what's best for me.

"'Newfound', what's that supposed to mean? If you'd been listening, you'd know it's the furthest thing from newfound!" I can't stop my voice from rising. I look away. "I've always been there for you, Yokolam – and you can't find the time to come to even one meeting?"

The sessions with the Women's Land Rights Cooperative have now been running for a year, and he hasn't come to a single one. "The stories we hear in those sessions would help you see why I need to be here."

"I wanted to come... but you know things at home haven't been easy – preparing to leave Mama here alone with that man."

His excuse doesn't make sense, but I'm tired of arguing with him.

"Anyway, don't you want more ... more for this organisation of yours? In Kampala there would be greater coverage and resourcing, don't you see?" He says this like one who's learned in the workings of the world, explaining it to someone who's still an outsider. He's rapidly starting to sound like one of the mzee in the village.

"You just need to accept that we will never agree on this. You see nothing here, and, well, I see so many reasons to stay. It's okay, just go to the city and leave us village people here in the village."

"Ah, Achen, stop with all of that! If you ask me, you just want to be different – to your own detriment. You can't fight reality forever."

I can't comprehend the words coming from his mouth, but what's more surprising is the expression on his face – like I'm the one being unreasonable. Frustration is starting to cloud his eyes.

"Sometimes I wonder who you are, Yokolam." The words escape my mouth, and though I know they'll pierce him, in this moment they are true.

"Let's go," he says aggressively, almost shouting.

I stand and we start making our way home. There are no words really left to say, so we walk together but separately. I can feel the pain of anger in my chest and my eyes are welling up – but no, I will not cry. I look away from him and at the bushes on the side of the road, so he doesn't notice my eyes. He's staring straight ahead, walking a little in front of me.

I want him to go to Kampala and study and do well. He's always been passionate about the law, human rights and justice. I hope this interest is entirely his and not just another attempt at being better than the Army Man.

We get to my compound, still no words between us. He walks ahead to greet Mama and the other elders, his face lighting up like nothing's happened between us. This switching on and off of emotions makes me deeply uncomfortable.

"Oh, my son!" Mama rushes to hug him, with the biggest smile on her face.

"Mama, so good to see you, so strong and beautiful."

"Ah no, an old woman like me!" she says, dusting her kitenge.

He smiles back. "The years don't seem to age you. You must tell us your secret."

Mama laughs fondly, placing her hand on his shoulder. "You're too kind for your own good."

"Mama. I'm just telling the truth."

They've always been so fond of each other. "You go well tomorrow and make us all proud, eh? You must come past for some sweet potatoes for the journey tomorrow morning." She hugs him tightly again before allowing him to continue on his way.

No goodbye. I just watch as he walks away from the compound. I know I'll regret not saying anything, but why can't he do it? He's the one who must apologise, after all.

Over the next few days, I miss him bitterly. I miss the most ordinary things, like how he says my name; the way he irritates me like no one else can. I could go in to the centre to phone him, but I don't.

The months that follow are filled with this tug of war: to call him or not? I can justify both. Until I just stop one day, because this never-ending wondering and uncertainty is too frustrating. I occupy my days instead with other things.

Although village life becomes more challenging as I get older, I'm grateful for those challenges. Days filled with playing and stories have been traded for a young adulthood of constant questioning. A desire to understand life more deeply.

A lot of the girls I was in secondary school with did not go on to further studies; they're all married, and have either given birth or are about to. It's now their loved ones and providing for them that consumes their days. I don't see much of Betty for this reason – she's one of those preparing for her kwanjula. These days have forced me to spend more time in solitude.

But I also grow more and more involved with the Women's Cooperative: my first cause. I read about activists speaking outright against the presidency, when it went back on its promise to provide sanitary pads to schoolgirls; about activists taking to social media, starting a crowdfunding initiative. I feel so encouraged. I spend my afternoons studying Wangari Muta Maathai and the Green Belt Movement. I love this idea of active citizenry, beginning with a small group of women and leading to sustainable development. Her slogan – "Communities mobilising and taking responsibility to address their needs" – injects courage into me.

I attend church, and walk home filled with the sense of purpose preached by Mama's priest. He paces around the stage, declaring: "God is in control, nothing is by chance. There is purpose in everything, even the place you are born." I believe it.

I know now what I want to do with my life. I am certain.

I haven't checked my emails in a month. I usually wait until I have a chance to go in to Nilo's shop; there's another internet café in the centre closer to home, but the owner charges exorbitant rates. And Nilo has become my friend.

I met Nilo by chance one day when Mama sent me to her tailor at the centre, to order a gomesi for someone's child's kwanjula ceremony. Mama insists on attending every function in the village; she says it's an investment one must make to ensure that people come to our compound too. The tailor wasn't there, and I was getting tired of waiting when I noticed a new shop across the road, with "Internet Café" in bold white writing against a blue background. It definitely hadn't been there the last time I was at the centre.

"What are you standing there for, come on, come in!"

The girl working in the shop had an inviting smile. I went

in, and we sat trading stories for a while. Nilo was originally from South Sudan – her smooth, jet-black skin gave this away – and new to the country. The shop, she told me, belonged to a lady living abroad who'd set up internet cafés all across Uganda. All part of "Silicon Savannah" – the East African economic boom. For myself, I hated how these "booms" were exclusionary, deciding which socioeconomic concerns were more important than others.

Nilo's shop has rods where all manner of printed material, newspapers and magazines are on display in perfectly straight lines. There's a wooden stool and table where Nilo's computer is placed, and three workstations opposite hers that are meant for the customers. There's a calendar on the wall, with a picture of a crested crane above the slogan, "Uganda, the Pearl of Africa".

Nilo is one of those people who's always smiling. She'll ask how you are, genuinely, and offer a helping hand. Time and time again I find myself volunteering information to her that I would normally only discuss with my closest friends; there's something about her calm that reminds me of Cynthia.

Nilo's family fled Sudan when the tribal lines were drawn between south and north. A lot of her extended family are still trapped in that country, now a warzone. She avoids conversations about the war, and I wonder if this is her way to cope with pain. Once, she mentioned that she prays every day, and hopes that God will hear her prayers. It's a strange thing – given where she comes from, being here is the best thing that could've happened to Nilo. I think of Yokolam and how he always wanted to leave; the relativity of things.

Today, I'm eager to open my emails. After a brief conversation with Nilo, I sit in front of the computer, unable to contain my excitement. I skim through the mails, excited to discover what each next line contains. I see Sandra and Cynthia's names, as expected – but there's nothing from Yokolam.

Sandra and Cynthia both left for university: Sandra's somewhere in London and Cynthia's in South Africa. Sandra, still her cynical self, writes about how pretentious the diaspora Africans in London are. She doesn't like her roommate, although she's trying to give her a chance. It's strange seeing her "spoilt" cousins – they didn't grow up together, and now Notting Hill on Sundays for lunch is a must. She smiles and tries to tolerate them. She seems happy, but profusely refusing to admit it. Politics, philosophy and economics – the PPE, it seems, are well suited to contain her.

Cynthia's in Port Elizabeth. She has a study visa but can't work. She needs to supplement her scholarship, though, so she's found a job as a waitress. It's not bad, she writes, but because the manager knows she doesn't have work papers and is desperate, he's exploiting her. "It's better than nothing, and the tips are good, even without a base salary," she says. Her air of goodwill is still there. She mentions a few people from our region who are now in Port Elizabeth too.

"The African foreign nationals in South Africa either lose their morals or become more devout in their faith," she writes. "Ah, Achen, the way some of these people are just out of control, their parents would be dumbfounded! I went to an East African Society party the other night. It's great to have met people, but man, was it wild!"

I savour their emails, realising how deeply I missed them. Our friendship is the meeting of three distinct personalities, strengthened by the fact that we simply allow each other to be who we are. We work well together, with minimal effort.

I write back, telling them that my new obsession is social rights activism, and that I've found my purpose. It's like finally finding the language to explain a feeling that's been growing in you for years. I tell them about Yokolam and me, and how he'd left.

As I press send, my mind immediately floods with all the other things I wanted to tell them. I miss the comfort of their companionship.

RED

Red is the colour of romance, of letters containing secret words that find their way past your eyes and into your heart. It is the strange tale of a stranger… whispers between white sheets, the language that hands and skin speak under skies full of stars. Red is passion. Red is not safe.

Nyakale

Ntombi and I walk to upper campus together to register for the first semester. We could take a shuttle, but there's something about being in a new place that awakens a sense of adventure in both of us. The campus looks breathtaking from this angle: clear blue skies, the mountain, green grass untainted by footsteps, the clouds precisely drawn.

"I can't believe we're here, starting the rest of our lives," Ntombi says, a determined look on her face.

"I know, right? It's exciting but also strange… we're like little birds, pushed out of our parents' nests."

"Nyakale, I like you, but you need to stop using metaphors in your everyday conversations." We both laugh.

Upper campus is full of crowds of people walking up and down. Some hurriedly, others casually, evidently delighted by their conversations. The beginnings of blooming friendships, the discovery of common interests. We start at the Humanities building, because Ntombi's convinced me that it only makes sense to start at the south end of campus, where she has to register. The building is filled with artists, politicians and philosophers. Vintage outfits, pants with turn-ups, dark lipstick: urban revolutionaries.

"Nyakale, these lines are ridiculous, perhaps you can wait for me there?" Ntombi points to a canteen not far away, with tables and chairs.

"Okay…" Already I can feel Uncle's impatience taking me over. "Let's see how long it takes?"

"Just text if you decide to leave," she says. I'm still shocked at how easygoing she is: nothing is ever too serious for more than a mellow response.

But after an hour of waiting, I'm starting to get a little agitated, tired of sitting, thinking and people-watching. Mid-thought, I feel a soft tap on my shoulder.

"Hi. Nyakale, right?"

Standing beside me is a grinning, athletic guy. His muscular legs are bowed into slight "brackets", and he has the haircut Kendrick Lamar made famous – skinny dreads, short on the sides. His overgrown beard gives him a unique look, coupled with round, brown-framed glasses. He's wearing loosely fitted, faded black jeans, an ironed white T-shirt and brown loafers. He has the kind of eyes that say a lot: they're on me like magnets, telling me he's already decided that this hello is the first of many.

I give him a goofy smile, searching my memories. "Umm… hello? You look familiar but I can't recall where I know you from," I finally say, embarrassed.

He smiles, a skew smirk that curls just the left side of his mouth. I can tell he's aware of his "boyish charm".

"Well, you wouldn't remember me, we weren't reeeally friends back then, but we went to the same high school. Does the class clown ring any bells?"

I think of all the guys in my matric class… this guy was definitely not one of them. I look at him intently and that's when I realise – it's him. The rugby first-team captain.

"What, waaaait, Lwazi?" This guy standing in front of me cannot be Lwazi from school!

"Hahaha, yes, it's me. Don't look so shocked – I've done my fair share of growing up and cleaning up. I hope!" It seems he's one of those people who laughs after every second word.

"Wait, so explain why the captain of the rugby first team is in the Humanities building," I tease him. "You were voted the most likely to become, hmmm, what was it again, a professional athlete?"

"Well, things went south in our matric year… I had a terrible injury towards the end of the season. Maybe you heard about it."

"Ah, how stupid of me. I didn't know it was that serious. Last time I saw you, it seemed like your Blue Bulls future was guaranteed."

"Don't worry about it, we all thought I would recover in time… but life has interesting plot twists."

"I'm so sorry Lwazi, I didn't realise."

"Stop, it's okay, really! I went to all these gruelling physio sessions and eventually it was pretty clear that my Blue Bulls dream wasn't going to happen. It was a life-altering moment. In a lot of ways." He pauses, still holding my gaze, and takes a breath. "I mean, I was forced to question who I was, without the tries and conversions. So, long story short, I fell in love with literature – well, philosophy. I'll be majoring in it, with African studies as a minor. I guess I want to make some sense of existential questions." He stops and smiles sheepishly. "Sorry for rambling on and on!"

"Wow. It seems like the last few years have been eventful," I say, surprised at how freely he's sharing these intimate details of his life. In fact, I struggle to hide my shock. This can't be Lwazi – not the annoying, arrogant Lwazi I remember!

Perhaps this is his attempt at reinvention. I can't wait to tell Aisha about this; she'll never believe me.

"Please tell me we can continue this conversation over lunch sometime in the week," he smiles. More a statement than a question – he's so certain the answer will be an immediate yes.

"I'll let you know," I say. I really should say no – but maybe, just maybe, we all deserve second chances. I'd be lying if I said the man's transformation wasn't an unexpected breath of fresh air – but I also can't forget that this is Lwazi! And what's that thing people say, about a leopard and its spots?

"Can I have your number, just so I can remind you to think through my tempting proposition?" he says with joking formality, his hand held out like he's asking me for a dance. The moment jogs my memory – that night at Sam's house; Lwazi forcefully nudging me to dance with him. But I hear the words "of course" come out of my mouth – so swiftly, without a fight.

He hands me his phone and takes mine, softly touching my fingers. Quickly he types in his number. "There you have it. Thank you Nyakale, it was so ... good to see you."

"Good to see you too."

I am astounded.

It's been some time since we last spoke, Aisha and I. There have been things weighing heavily on each of us, and eventually between us. And talking about it sometimes feels like it gives these things a life.

Still, it is one of life's greatest pleasures, this kind of friendship, where each conversation ends in an unsaid comma but never a full stop. Since we were six, even before we knew grazed knees were not the worst kind of pain in the world, Aisha was the one who'd plaster my knee when I fell. Rub my back, rubbing and sometimes laughing my tears away. Our souls always dancing in harmony, like we'd lived through all these moments before. With the years, though, our pain has evolved; and we've learnt that, even with plasters, there are times rose-petals of blood refuse to be hidden.

"Hi Aisha, I can't seem to see your face?" I'm really excited to Skype her. I love seeing the expressions she makes while I update her on my life.

I hear her fidgeting in the background. "I don't know, it may be the network."

"How are you? I miss you so much!" I say. But I feel a vacancy in my heart.

"I'm okay, I guess. I guess thinking we would talk every week was a bit unrealistic."

"Tell me about Wits. How's it been? And you will not in your wildest dreams believe who I bumped into!" The words pour out of my mouth.

"Mmm, Wits, it's all right, I'm adjusting. Medicine might not have been my worst idea, after all. Tell me, tell me, tell me who you saw?"

"Lwazi!"

"Oh my god, the comedian-meets-jock-meets-the-patriarchy?"

"Well, it seems like he and who he used to be are complete strangers. He's studying, wait for it... philosophy."

"Oh, my goodness, that is absolutely bizarre! What are the chances?" She giggles.

"Wait, there's more – he asked to take me to lunch and I told him I'd think about it. We even exchanged numbers. Yep!"

We laugh and laugh at the irony of it all. In the midst of this nonsensical laughter, I want to ask Aisha how she really is, but fear overpowers my words.

"AisHaaaaa... AisHaaaaa... AisHaaaa!" It's her mother in the background, calling in a slurred voice. She bursts into Aisha's room. Unsteady on her feet, loudly demanding that Aisha bring her Mbali's favourite teddy bear.

Aisha is embarrassed – but it's me here. I wish she knew she doesn't have to be embarrassed with me. She doesn't say anything, just dutifully stands up. Her mother leans on her shoulder and Aisha ushers her out of the room. I hear a loud clatter, followed by soft voices. After a few minutes, Aisha reappears.

"Is everything okay?" A stupid question that I ask nonetheless.

"Yes, of course, everything's fine. Tell me more about seeing Lwazi and everything."

We speak these days, but we no longer really talk. And maybe this is why I haven't called in a while.

Lwazi calls and asks if I've thought about it, the lunch date. He tells me he's come to the obvious conclusion, which is that we should hang out at the Old Biscuit Mill Saturday market.

There are numerous reasons not to go. But my suspicion is mixed with a heaped tablespoon of curiosity – what would it be like, to spend my Saturday with him? My mind slowly begins to oppose rational theories with fantasies about his wildly skewed smile and his laughing eyes.

We sit on the ground at the Biscuit Mill, sipping on red-berry cocktail concoctions in glass jars. Lwazi talks a lot and easily about his family from the Eastern Cape: his father, whom he wouldn't recognise even if he passed him on the street. Bhuti Khaya, his mother's youngest brother, who's always been a father figure to him. His little sister Anita, who is partly responsible for the glow in his eyes. He speaks with fondness lacing every word about his selfless single mother, and how he wants to take the entire world off its axis and hand it to her one day. The weight of being talented at sport, and then constantly being expected to "man up", whatever society deems that to mean on any given day.

I look up into Lwazi's eyes. Below his unrestrained eyebrows, an entire world lives in that gaze: curiosity to understand; contentment in this moment. When he speaks of the things that grip him, his eyes sparkle like he might cry. I wonder if they look this way when he wakes up, or just before he falls asleep.

I'm a little afraid of how I'm already drawn in by the mysteries of his world, by the things he's lived through and experienced. I'm afraid the more he tells, the more I'll want to know, falling into the kind of love that knowledge of another breeds.

I can't wait to do nothing with him today, I think as I walk up to his res. The reception area is empty, light-coloured bare walls making it seem even more vacant. Exams are around the corner, and I guess that explains the silence.

I walk down the passage to Lwazi's room. My lip quivers, and I bite some sense into it. As I knock on his door, I notice that my hand has forgotten how to steady itself. On my third knock, I hear: "Cooooooooming!"

He appears at the door, his smile complete and arms ready to give me one of those lingering teddy-bear hugs.

In his room, his blue bedding is neatly laid out. No crease in sight. I sit on his bed, shoes off and legs pulled towards my chest. He sits on the floor on the grey fluffy rug, next to a messy pile of books, large books balanced on top of small ones, so it looks like it could tumble any minute. From previous visits, I've managed to deduce that the heap consists of philosophy, politics, history, and others I am yet to decipher.

"So how are you?" he asks.

"I'm okay, it's just been one of those incredibly tiring weeks, you know."

"Noooo, that's not good enough!" he says in a theatrical voice. "How are you? I don't want the empty bones of answers! Where's the detail, Kale?"

I look at him and smile. He started calling me Kale the morning we became "official". We were having breakfast at my apartment. I've always had an attachment to sitting around a table for breakfast. I don't know – something to do with the importance of pausing before the day has its way with you.

Lwazi is not one to beat around the bush. Between sips of orange juice and bites of flapjack, he looked up and said, "I think we are a good thing; and good things don't come by very often, so they must be explored. No objections? I thought not."

I couldn't help but laugh and kiss him.

And now here I am, lying on his bed. "Tell me about your week?"

"How have I not told you?! I'm reading this book about Thomas Sankara – this man, Kale, he was probably Africa's Greatest."

I smile at his theatrics.

"No, listen, he increased literacy in Burkina Faso in four years from thirteen to seventy-three per cent. Reduced corruption, refused to use state money for himself. He even planted trees!"

"What? How did we not learn about this man in history lessons?"

"I know, right? It's all these hidden figures."

He joins me on the bed, lying next to me with his feet loosely hanging off the end, Thomas Sankara's biography in hand. "In other news, Kale..." he gazes at me. "Are you still adamant about the sex and marriage thing? I'm just asking – not at all trying to sway you."

Once more, I have to laugh. "Lwazi, you know my take on it. It's sacred, the meeting of not just bodies but souls – so yes, I am. That's not changing. Your philosophical brain should understand this."

"Okay fine, you win," he says, standing up and dramatically throwing his hands in the air.

I didn't meet Lwazi that first time, back when we were at school and he asked me to dance. I met him the moment he said, "Sorry for rambling on and on," and I sat fascinated by the different emotions his face wore with each word. So much of who he was unpacked and on display, just for me. I met him in the moments he looked away and I wondered where he went. And when I'd met him in all these small moments, I knew: gosh, I love this man.

Ntombi and I, too, have formed a bond I can't quite explain. Despite contrasting views, we have somehow managed to forge a deep appreciation for each other. It's odd, and most of our other friends find it odd too. I can't for the life of me recall when it happened. Was it the junk food and movie nights? When she had a crush and I listened? Or when we told each other our deepest secrets?

Ntombi went to one of the best schools in KwaZulu-Natal, St Anne's Diocesan College – a fact she'll casually mention, not getting the fuss. Her father's a renowned businessman and her mother lives in Switzerland, where she works for a humanitarian organisation. The most obvious differences between us are Ntombi's personally assisted life and her father's black card. She has zero reservations about people knowing the extent of her family wealth. She always playfully insists that she'll cover the bills – and she does.

What draws me to her? It's not about the wealth, but it's the disregard she has for what people think of her. She lives the best way she knows how, given what she has. I, on the other hand, tread too carefully. Everything calculated, suppressing myself so others can feel comfortable. Which at first might seem noble, but could also be conceit.

A cold Thursday night. We've been in the library: him studying for his philosophy paper, and me working on an economics assignment. Now we stand shivering at West bus-stop on upper campus; thirty minutes have passed and still no shuttle in sight. My hands are freezing. I'm wearing his black Kopano hoody and his arms are around me, making sure I'm warm – because he is an "Alpha male", constantly asserting his manhood by being my protector. I let this slip because yes, it's thoughtful, and perhaps I am guilty of over-analysing the situation.

Why doesn't the bloody shuttle come? Minutes turn into an hour, and he suggests that it only makes sense for him to walk me down to my studio apartment in Rondebosch, on the corner next to the railway.

I'm nervous, I don't know why. These unreliable bus schedules. He walks me to the door, as usual. Each time, we go through the age-old argument, where he attempts to climb the walls I've built to keep distance between us. He wants in, and this night my protests fall on deaf ears. It's drizzling and the wind is cold. Surely, I can't let him walk back in the rain.

Inside, we continue our habitual ritual: discussing philosophy.

"Kale, bear with me for a minute: self-reliance. Emerson is fascinating on this concept. If self-actualisation occurs at a large scale, the result is positive externalities for society at large. Yes!" His eyes sparkle and there's a satisfied look on his face.

"Self-actualisation? You mean self-absorption," I tease.

"You, my love, are missing the point. It's more self-acceptance, and as a result of self-acceptance, a heightened sense of existence. My job is done here, haha!" He's always speaking and laughing simultaneously.

One of the most attractive things about Lwazi is how he shares random facts about the world with me. Anything from discussing how astronauts brush their teeth in space, to precisely dissecting injustice – and always with an intense look in his eyes. He has a need to change things, to make things better. It appeals to the very same feeling in me, and my fear of oblivion. We're both consumed by a passion for life – and it combusts when we're together.

There is no couch in my typical student studio apartment. Minutes turn into hours as our conversation travels between different subjects. I sit on my bed, eyes heavy; but I will open them. Next minute, it's not just me but us on my bed, in each other's arms. So close that I'm not sure if I'm hearing his heart beating or mine.

I wake up unsettled, rays coming through the dull grey curtains to land on my eyes. I'm disorientated – why is Lwazi here? Unfamiliar but also comfortable.

This, then, will become our norm. We don't have sex, but it's another road crossed that we have no business crossing, stop signs ignored in my head, both consciously and unconsciously.

It's raining thick droplets, the kind that arrive first to announce the coming of a storm.

Today is our second anniversary. I just got off the phone with him – we've been talking to each other all night. Reminiscing: first impressions, first kisses, first dates, first birthdays, first fights, all the firsts. The past couple of years feel like an eternity of love. It's 6 am and my eyes are bloodshot – always happens when I don't get enough sleep. I finally close my eyes, memories making for a comfortable pillow. I'm sure I'm smiling, feeling so awkwardly silly. I hear the doorbell just as dreams are on the horizon. I stumble out of bed to see who's at the door.

"Lwazi!" I exclaim, sleepy but still excited to see him. "What are you doing here?"

"Hi Kale, I had to see your face before I go to campus."

I blush like it's my first time hearing him use these words on me, in that husky tone accompanied by a laugh. I feel nervous, off-balance – and I'm not a girl who falls easily. I am quite steady on my own two feet, but he makes butterfly wings flutter in my stomach and my mind turns into jelly.

In his hand is a green shopping bag, which he puts down on my kitchen counter. "When do I get to see you today, Kale?"

I love how he says this – like he's not seeing me right now. "Well, I have to go to middle campus to talk to Francine, she wants to discuss the direction of my essay."

"Before you go off on a tangent about your essay, I'll be seeing you at eight tonight – and don't ask where we're going."

How easily he makes me smile. "Where are you taking me? Come on, tell me!"

"Woman, let me surprise you for once," he teases.

On any other day, that remark would lead to me lecturing this boy, I mean man, but today I just grin. Before I walk him out, I peek into the shopping bag, and in it are all my favourite things: cranberry juice, flapjacks, honey, strawberries. I playfully push him against the wall and kiss him.

"Thank you, my favourite," I whisper into his ear.

After he's gone, his Bulgari cologne lingers all over my apartment. It's one of my favourite smells – like Lwazi, it's daring, simple yet layered.

I go back to bed for another hour or so. I'm exhausted, but Francine will be livid if I miss our meeting. Francine is one of the smartest women I've ever come across: articulate, carelessly treading the line between confidence and arrogance. Knowledgeable to the point of irritating her colleagues, she knows a thing or two about everything.

In the shower, today the only thoughts my mind chooses to entertain are of Lwazi. White picket fences, us the perfect, most unlikely match, and the world ours for the taking.

No! I glance at the clock, it's already ten past eight. How am I going to get dressed, eat breakfast and get to middle campus by nine? Okay, no time to think of an outfit. I grab my black dress, black stockings, my maroon jersey, and the scarf Aunty Mercy got me from Uganda. Nostalgia briefly erupts as I wrap it loosely around my neck. I finally get to middle campus and Francine's office just as the clock strikes nine. Technically, I'm late: she has this theory that five minutes early is on time.

Francine is Italian, but has lived all over Africa. Her diplomat parents started moving when she was five, and she went to more schools than she can count on two hands. Cum laude from Harvard in economics and law, then an MBA and a PhD in African studies, the cherry on top of her accomplishments. Let's just say she's a notch above genius.

She's poised, with an unshakeable certainty when she speaks. When she walks into a room, people gravitate to her. I remember being astonished at how she doesn't do that humble "I'm-not-so-great" thing when people compliment her or comment on her accomplishments. She uses words like "phenomenal" to describe herself, and leans in to the praise. I've noticed how this often makes people inhale sharply and shuffle in their seats, especially the women.

I once told her that I wanted to be like her some day, if I was fortunate enough. She shrugged her shoulders, unimpressed, a thoughtful smile on her face.

"Nyakale, things are never what they seem. Never easy, not a wish away."

I asked her what that meant.

"We see half the story, Nyakale. If you'd seen the story in its entirety, then maybe I would agree with you wanting to be like me."

I still wonder what things she was thinking about but not mentioning.

Now she's slowly pacing around her office. Through the windows, you can see the mountain and blue sky. She has a pen in her hand that she's tapping rhythmically against my printed-out essay. My audacious topic: 'The relationship between economic growth and unemployment reduction in sub-Saharan Africa'.

"So, Nyakale, you do realise this paper has the potential to be brilliant. I'm impressed by the way your passion reflects in how you've constructed your arguments – and as you know, I'm not easily impressed," she says, gracefully gliding from one corner of her office to the next. "I think an extension of this would work beautifully for your Honours dissertation. For your Masters, you'll have to decide on either contrasting African regions or specific countries... that would make sense for your data gathering, yes?" Her voice is as calm as ever, but I can see she's excited.

I smile shyly. "Yes, that's the plan – expand it to more countries, and eventually the world! Well, Africa," I laugh.

She finally sits at her desk and grabs her red pen, dissecting my essay line by line. Never giving me easy answers, but always asking the right questions. We talk at length about economics, all its facets. How it's exclusionary. How it doesn't hold constant in real life. How complexity and theory are like oil and water.

Aisha is in Cape Town for the week for some clinic practicals. I'm meeting her, Mufasa and Nina for lunch. The wind is blowing gently for a change, not its usual unruly self, which I've become accustomed to in this city. It's a beautiful spring afternoon in September and the trees on Lover's Walk are transitioning, somewhere between the browns of leaves gone and the green of life, clothing them in a hopeful aura.

I'm thinking of Lwazi, of how he's evolved from the jock I could barely tolerate into this man. This conscious man, edging towards being toxically consumed by the injustices of the world, and his responsibility for them. It frightens me that I'm quickly changing into the girl I once mocked. The girl so invested in a relationship that she ceases to be a separate entity.

The streets are empty as most students have already gone home for the vacation. I'll probably leave for home next week. It's exhausting that my friends still ask me why I haven't visited Uganda. I'm crossing fingers that no one will bring this up at lunch today. They think the fact that I have a twin in Uganda who I've never spoken to is the most absurd thing. What's a little frightening is that I don't think about her often anymore, not nearly as much as when I was younger. I remember Aunty Mercy sending me a picture of them; I looked at it and I wanted to feel something, anything – but there was nothing left to feel. The woman was Achen's mother, and Achen was a girl who looked disturbingly like me but was galaxies away. A stranger. There are days I wish this wasn't true, that instead our story was like a novel – one with a happy ending.

On the taxi, I observe the passengers. For as long as I can

remember; people have fascinated me – the fact that each one has a unique inner life. I love to imagine who they are: how they got here, how their facial expressions are an extension of how they feel. My eyes and mind conspiring, speculating, drawing what could be unfounded conclusions.

There are three older mamas in the back of the taxi. They look like today has stripped their souls bare; their faces remind me of the helpers and nannies I used to see on my walk to school. In the row in front of the mamas, there are three cool kids, the epitome of fashion-forward on campus at the moment: crop tops, high-waist denims, and black-and-white Nike Roshe Run sneakers. Next to me is a gentleman, the suit type – the kind who looks like his mind consists of markets and merger and acquisition deals. Back straight, fitted navy suit, skinny grey tie, white cotton shirt and of course Happy Socks. The driver is coloured, with a scar under his eye. The kind of scar that has a story to accompany it.

"Sisi, sicela itshintshi!" one mama exclaims from the back seat. The girl in front of me is frantically counting coins and sending the change to the back.

"Shoprite stop!" the driver shouts.

"Yes driver," I reply.

I try to speak quickly, just audibly. I've learnt to only say what's essential, avoiding the judgment I've received numerous times for being black and speaking English in a taxi. That's when I wish Aisha had spoken Zulu more often around me – but her dad being Tanzanian complicated things.

I get off at Shoprite, cross the road and walk around towards the Food Lovers' Market. Upstairs on the balcony, I see Aisha sitting with Nina and Mufasa: laughter and glasses of wine. Mufasa's probably sharing the latest on structural engineering, and how his kind of degree is superior to any other.

"Finally, Kale!" they exclaim, and the endless laughter begins. We talk love, family, politics; in between, casually throwing teasing insults at each other. Nina with the constant boy drama – she somehow always falls for the typical bad boy.

It feels like the darkness has lifted from Aisha. She mentions Mbali at moments in conversation, but her posture doesn't change; instead, her eyes light up, and a smile of nostalgic fondness emerges on her face. She protests Mufasa's adamant belief that Engineering is the God of degrees: "I will spend the rest of my life saving lives. You simply cannot beat that, and attempting to do so would be inhumane."

We all scream, "Unfair!" and burst into laughter.

I watch Aisha, taking her in. It's so good to have her back. I feel slightly selfish for thinking this, but it is. I reach over and place my hand on her shoulder, and I feel her exhale, like she's settling back into herself.

I cannot wait to see Lwazi later. I am slightly nervous.

Okay, so definitely my black dress, with the ocean-blue heels; then there's still my makeup and hair. In between getting ready, I keep reaching for my phone, reading his chain of text messages.

I hear the doorbell. Lwazi is early. "Come in," I call. I still need to finish putting on my makeup.

The door is unlocked, he lets himself in, comes through to my room and kisses me on my forehead. "Happy anniversary, my favourite human. I love you a ridiculous amount of love," he says.

"Come on, stop – you know I'm already yours, right?" I tease.

"You know how lucky you are to have me, Kale, the rays to your sun?" he says. He's poured two glasses of white wine, and is chuckling in between sips.

I'm sitting in front of the mirror, trying not to be distracted by his stare. Just as I apply my dark-red matte lipstick, he leans over and steals a kiss, smudging my lipstick. I keep glancing at his silhouette in the mirror. His bronze skin and dark bold features. This attempt at flawless makeup becomes more and more futile. He keeps coming to steal kisses. His lips against mine feel like the first sip of water after a long day. He starts tickling me.

"Lwazi!" I protest, between giggles and squeals. "We're going to be late for our reservation at the restaurant!"

We are rolling on the floor, playfully fighting, the perfect combination of lovers and friends. He keeps tickling me, every inch of my body. I'm giggling hysterically and just as I'm about to let out another laugh, he looks at me – a look I've never seen before. He sees me and kisses me; I shiver, feeling the adrenalin in my veins – I'm high on this boy. He kisses my neck, my ears. His kisses like petals landing gently in all the right places. I know we shouldn't go any further, but the protests and my sanity get lost somewhere between him holding me tightly and his warm breath lingering on my neck. His body on mine is warm, all-consuming; in that moment all other things are reduced to nothing.

His hands are discovering my body like uncharted territory, but he seems to know just where to go. He takes off my dress, getting any unnecessary barrier out of the way. My melanin-rich skin against his paler shade – this is art. He unclips my bra, like he's done this a thousand times. I'm wondering how many girls he's had in this very position. For me, he's the first to travel this far.

He whispers in my ear, "I love you, Kale."

His breath against my skin, so warm. His hands in between my legs, stroking my thighs gently, creeping higher. I grab his hand… but my body is miles ahead of my mind.

He is inside me. Wait, he is inside me. My body, astonished, sends shock signals to my brain. Is this because my mind and body are finally in agreement that we should not be doing this? My mind is blank; I am here, heightened feelings expelling all rational thought, but I'm frozen. Just lying here.

Tonight the storm arrived. It is pouring, bountiful amounts of water – no gentle drip-drop on the window pane, but instead the overwhelming sounds of water being poured by the gallon on the roof. Thunder and lightning, my heart beating in my ear so loudly it feels like my chest is on the verge of exploding. Lwazi lying naked next to me is as peaceful as a baby, although there's a storm raging right next to him. A million thoughts a second run through my mind. How did we get here? How did I get here? When did I make this decision?

My moral claims dissolve along with the idea that this was a "forever" thing. There's no ring on my finger, and this is no honeymoon night. Just another deflowered girl for him and his friends to discuss, as guys do. I hate him in this moment. I hate that I gave it to him and he took it from me, that he owns a piece of me. I do not know the person lying next to Lwazi, I think to myself. I am not her. I am the girl who does not do things like this. I thought I was better than those girls, the ones who should be lying here. I am sorry.

I have barely slept; my eyes are blood red and puffy, and they hurt as though I've been crying the whole night. My body aches like it's at war with itself. I'm hoping he isn't awake – and no, he isn't. I get up, put on my favourite grey sweatpants and my white jersey and my red scarf, the one from Aunty Mercy, because today I need some grounding. I need a home far away from this moment.

I walk out of my apartment, leaving a note for Lwazi to leave the keys under the pot plant just outside the door. I walk aimlessly up the road, with no idea where I'm going. All I know is that I need to get away from here, from him. To clear my head, make some sense of this, of it. I feel as though people are looking at me, as though they know I've broken this vow to myself: a traitor, another conquest. I finally sit down at a tiny coffee shop, hoping the hours will drift away. I just need him to be gone by the time I get back home. Minutes turn into hours: people-watching, reading the newspaper, occupying my mind with anything that takes me away from thoughts of last night, thoughts of him, thoughts that keep trying to break their way past these self-constructed bars. All at once, going home seems to be the only sane thought my mind can construct.

"Hi Aunty Mercy, how are you?" Just sound normal, just sound normal. My eyes burn with shame.

"Hello, my baby! I'm faring fine, thank you. What's the matter? You sound a little down?"

"It's nothing, you worry too much. I've been walking, that's probably why my voice sounds strange. By the way, I'm thinking about coming home tonight – well, the bus will only arrive midday tomorrow, is that okay?"

"Of course, Kale, you know how boring and quiet the house is without you here with me and your uncle!"

I smile, thinking of Aunty Mercy and Uncle's countless debates about how I turned out; the two of them laughingly wondering who raised me. "I love you, Aunty. Please send my greetings to Uncle."

"I love you, Nyakale. Let us know when you leave, and call me as soon as you're about to arrive. We are so excited to see you."

There's never been a deficit of love. I have always known that Aunty Mercy and Uncle love me deeply, sacrificially. The kind of love that only parenting evokes.

Back at my apartment, I hold my breath as I gently lift the pot plant, hand anxiously scavenging for the key. I let out a sigh of relief when I retrieve it.

I think of calling Aisha, but with all the things she's had to deal with lately, my dilemma seems insignificant. I know she'll listen, but she's carrying more than enough burdens. I put on some music, turning the speakers to maximum volume – anything to keep my mind occupied. Cleaning all of a sudden feels like I good idea. I start mopping, scrubbing every corner that's within reach, until my body and mind fall into a lull of exhaustion. I grab my phone to set an alarm: I need to wake up and pack. I can't afford to miss the bus later tonight.

Ten missed calls from Lwazi, and text messages I have no

intention of reading. I shut my eyes tightly. Just as I'm on the verge of dreams, my phone rings. It's him.

"Kale, I've been worried sick about you! How could you just leave – no call, no text, nothing. You can't just ghost on me, come on. Seriously!"

I'm quiet, thinking what to say – or maybe silence just feels easier than fighting. "Okay, I'm sorry. That's what you want me to say, right?" These are the words that escape my mouth at last. Feeble, lifeless words. "Lwazi, I'm going home tonight – my bus leaves at midnight. I just need to go home."

"Wait, what? But we were meant to spend the rest of this week together – that was the plan, Kale! You don't get to just go."

I pause again, taken aback by those words: You don't get to.

"Selfish – only thinking of yourself, Lwazi. I can't believe you're making this such a big deal. I'm going home just five days earlier than we'd planned. That can't be criminal."

"Fine, just be safe, okay? And let me know once you're home, Kale, you know I…"

I hang up before he can tell me that he loves me. I don't want to have to say it back. I'm not sure exactly what this feeling is. It's still all-consuming, but I am no longer sure it's love.

I get to the bus stop an hour before the bus is meant to arrive. My mind is preoccupied, but I'm thinking of nothing specific. It's the strangest feeling, this sweeping discomfort I can't shake off. I guess it's loss – this feeling of having given up something that culturally was never meant to be given away, except in the safe confines of marriage. Does this change who I am, my place in the world? I don't know, but I know that it isn't what a "nice girl" would do.

The lines at the bus station are long. The waiting area is small, congested and stuffy. In front of me is a young family. I'm guessing the mother is travelling alone – her two children are standing around, hugging her repeatedly. The older son is attempting to convince the younger ones that it's time to go, but each time he ushers them away, they escape his grip and run back to their mother's open arms.

We're finally en route, though the bus feels like it's hardly moving. Behind me is a woman and her baby – chubby and delighted as babies should be, with no concern in the entire world. I'm sitting here hoping that in the next twenty-odd hours she will not have to change the baby's nappy. I put in my earphones – the world-wide signal that I'm in no mood for small talk.

The joy of travelling at night is that the world seems at peace with itself, the weight of everything a lot more bearable. I feel a sadness settle, a known sadness – and that's how I can tell it isn't about Lwazi. Sadness arrives with friends: the thoughts neatly stored in parts of my mind I don't visit often come back like a flood.

I want my mother today. For her to tell me it's okay and wipe away my tears. I want my sister to be the person I call. I want to retrieve all the years we have lost. And I want my piano, to watch the keys dance for a few minutes as the world stands absolutely still. I want home.

I wake up to the smell of Aunty Mercy's millet porridge. These are the simple joys of being home, with no responsibility. Unfortunately, I still don't get to sleep in late. Aunty Mercy and Uncle are as diligent about us all sitting down for breakfast as when I still lived at home.

"Morning Kale," Aunty says, the biggest smile on her face. "Kale, come here and let me see you properly, you seem to have lost weight, my child – what are these studies doing to you?"

I laugh. It is these simple things that sing me lullabies and chase my self-loathing thoughts away.

"Aunty Mercy, you worry too much. I promise I am as healthy as any other student."

Uncle glances up from his newspaper. "You are welcome home, my daughter, we are so glad to have you with us. This daughter of ours, who only chooses to visit this house every now and then, like it's not her own." He smiles warmly, but I know he's being serious about wanting me to come home more often. I go over and hug him before sitting at the table.

Aunty Mercy places cassava, sweet potatoes, eggs and chicken livers on the table. All the things they would eat if they were still in Uganda.

"Let's bow our heads," Uncle says in a reverent tone. "Most gracious Father in Heaven, we thank you for this food. We thank you even for life itself, and how we are truly spoilt by you. Also, we thank you for bringing this child of ours, who gets lost, back home."

Aunty Mercy and I open our eyes and grin at each other.

"Amen," he concludes.

We pass around the different dishes, and I wait for the inevitable questions that must come before I can settle into the comfortable oblivion of vacation. Aunty Mercy begins cautiously: "Kale, are you still friends with that Lwazi boy?" It's a territory she treads gently; I assume she's caught between curiosity and a fear of really knowing. This is why she calls him a friend, fully knowing that he's more than that. Uncle tenses up, his brows crumpling; but he plays no part in such conversations.

I respond reluctantly, "Yes, I guess so."

I nod, convincing myself that yes, Lwazi and I still exist as this formidable unit, eagerly running towards life. Images of the future, the one that should be, gather like flashes of lightning in my mind: doing our Masters, then working for developmental organisations in the same city. Travelling the world. Discussing books together. Lwazi and me.

Uncle breaks into my thoughts with the next compulsory conversation: "So, Nyakale, you will be joining us working citizens after next year. You need to start thinking through which companies are possible options."

I smile meekly, knowing that in Uncle's mind is lodged a list of companies I could work for; the ones he would be proud to mention at business gatherings – a stamp that I was raised well. But I know that I don't want to do what's expected of me, just for the sake of it. I want something unorthodox. I can't decipher why I'm not swept up in it all – the appeal of the concrete jungle. I can't be one of those people who anxiously waits for Friday, and with equal intensity dreads Monday mornings.

"Well, Uncle, I'm still not sure if this is what I want to do, I mean—"

"Nyakale," he interjects, "please explain to me what there is to not be sure of? Say the word and I can put you in touch with people in any of these companies. I mean, in our times, Nyakale, your Aunty and I could not even begin to dream of such things. Don't forget where we come from."

There it is – the constant expectation hanging over my head. Where we come from, this piece of history that I am not even part of that predefines me; that dictates that I work harder, be better, be smarter. I have lived my life not only for myself, but for the missed opportunities of Aunty and Uncle; for my cousins barred from a "better life"; and for the sleeping corpses that house my ancestors' dreams. It has meant endless gratitude for these greener pastures. But who says this is better? What if I would have been as happy there, with my real mother? Silently, I nod.

Uncle sits up, his eyes haunted by memories of the past, and continues with a stern clarity in his voice: "Nyakale, but this uncertainty of yours, this indecision – these are all well and good, but they are luxuries. You're just starting out. Maybe later you can do these other things that interest you."

I wonder if I would have seen the world any differently if I'd grown up in their world. My mind drifts to Achen, wondering whether these thoughts are really as Uncle says, "luxuries".

I start clearing the table. It's a Saturday, so Aunty Mercy

and Uncle place themselves on the sofa in the living room, their Saturday ritual. Each of them picks a book from the assortment on the table. Uncle has I Write What I Like firmly in his hand, already engrossed, and Aunty Mercy picks up a book by Oprah and begins to page through it. Before me is one of the most mesmerising images I know; one that's become synonymous with home. It's the way Uncle and Aunty Mercy's bodies are so gently tilted towards one another. Their hands gently brushing; their soft, affectionate tones. It's how they're so captivated by literature, and simultaneously absorbed by each other's presence. Theirs is a comfortable love, a love not wanting but one satisfied. I drift to thoughts of Lwazi. This is not our love. Our love is restless, always wanting more.

We sit on opposite ends of the room, my heart beating like a drum. Lwazi stares out of the window, not saying a word.

How did we get here? How did I get here? I don't need to search my mind to find the moments, the wrong turns on roads we had no business treading. The kisses that lingered too long, hands that slipped too low below the waist. When Lwazi teased me about these morals of mine that belonged in bygone times. But he respected my choices – or was respect a word his tongue used loosely, between sweet nothings?

I can't recall the exact moment it happened, the moment my unquestioned moral truths became more like theories. I still believe that marriage and sex are sacred – but he was always the exception. Like most girls, I had a number of boxes a guy had to tick – no exceptions on that list of mine. Lwazi came nothing near that square-shouldered, tailored-suit, says-grace-before-a-meal guy I'd dreamt of. But he made me feel less afraid in the world and of the world, and I loved that. I couldn't have known that he'd come to be my favourite voice on the other end of a call. My favourite laugh, my favourite mystery, an enigma. I secretly relished the fact that he was made of puzzle pieces that I grappled to fit together. We were perfectly imperfect.

And me? Feminist meets religious meets issues, with

perhaps a hint of saviour mentality. Perhaps I, too, was not what he'd always imagined.

Achen

Since Yokolam left for the city, along with all my other peers, the village has become quieter; the things I never used to notice have become even louder. The young children given away to older men as wives, in exchange for cattle for their family. Then these children having children. Children not in school, but instead participants in an adulthood that isn't really theirs to live. The things that happen when the darkness descends that no one talks about. I've always known that it's a hard thing being a woman here – how a woman's motions are expected to be limited to nodding in agreement.

I guess these are some of the things that made Yokolam want to run for the hills and never look back. It is here that we struggled to see eye to eye, because these are the things that make me want to stay.

"Achen, leave these things alone!" Mama scolds.

"Mama, but for how long have we done that? Don't you think it's time for someone to say it's enough? Enough of this customary law, where men own all the land – and call it our culture, that must be preserved."

"Achen, how are you speaking like this, defying not only our culture but also the natural law of things? I think you are forgetting yourself, my child." Mama's voice strains as it rises.

But a switch in me has gone off, and all the words chained to my larynx have broken free. They are like wild beasts running free, rebellious. I can no longer hide the things that keep me awake when the black sky is pulled across the light.

"No. I am only beginning to find my tongue, Mama. I know the reason the women are in our compound is because they were chased away from their own homes. Mama, how much more space is there for you to house people, and when will you stop biting your tongue? This thing we are doing here isn't sustainable. Things need to change."

"I don't know where you have learnt these manners, Achen. I just don't know. What I do know is I didn't raise this defiance in my house."

I hear her, but my exhaustion had surpassed the point of retreat.

I spend the next few days moving from village to village on my bicycle, talking to the women. It shocks me that some are reluctant to speak to me about their plight, instead chasing me away before their husbands can see them talking to "the young girl who's decided to become the village vigilante".

"Leave it alone" – words I've become accustomed to hearing. But that is no longer an option.

I'm spending two weeks in the city, visiting Yokolam. The place makes me tense. The people here seem anxious – particularly about how they measure up to one another.

"Girl, what do you think of my outfit?" This is a sincere question among the young women in Yoko's circle of friends.

"You're a goddess."

"What a babe!"

They take turns going around the circle, exaggerating a little more with each compliment. The girl who asked the question now beaming in delight: "Ah, come on guys, these old clothes?"

I've never understood this – being too concerned about what others think; speaking on cue, not truthfully but to delight. The girls rehearse what to say to boys they like – this is foreign to me. In the village you just speak, no rehearsals; there's no time to construct life before living it.

And simple things seem to bother them in the city. Always impatient, always complaining about how things could be better. I've never seen complaining make such friends of people as I have here. Everyone in too much of a rush to say please and thank you, or even "How are you?" – and mean it. I wonder if contentment exists anywhere on these street corners. I look up at the bright city lights that make spotting a single star in the sky a rarity. Yes, the city is far more developed than the village, but I'm not sure I'm ready to make the trade.

Outside my own inner circle of girlfriends, I'm not good at this, at blending in. I say things like: "Oh, is it?" and "Sure," just so his friends don't think I'm uninterested. I don't know why he left me here alone with them.

"I'm tired, Achen, of this suffering – and for what?"

His eyes search mine, looking for an ally in his exhaustion. I look back at him, confused. I don't know when he became this way, always tired, the cynicism in his eyes a shield against any talk of hope.

Yokolam wants more and more. I, on the other hand, believe in having just enough. If we can have enough dignity for everyone, then this is a world I can live in. I worry that, unconsciously, we can become the things we fear the most – and in his eyes, lately, I see the Army Man.

"It's being here, Yokolam, it adds to this tiredness of yours. Only two weeks and I can tell why you're tired. Kampala is bustling with crowds of people struggling for money in a city with limited resources, that still reminds you daily with its extravagant shops of all the things you want and can't afford. You just need a week in the village," I tease.

He furrows his brow in irritation. "I hate when you do this, Achen. Always pretending there's no good in the city, just because you don't understand it. Has the village changed in the last thirty years? Has it?"

"It has! Well, maybe not in leaps and bounds, but soon it will. I must tell you about the Cooperative. We're currently signing petitions and planning for a women's rally right here in Kampala, so these city officials understand the seriousness of this matter." I hold my fist in the air, mimicking the defiance of a liberation hero. But he doesn't smile.

"Achen, these marches and petitions never change things. Don't you see that the only way to break out from the village and its backwardness is education? Then money, the currency of influence. I know how the law works and how it works here." His voice is laced with anger.

In front of me is the Army Man. A man married to three women; a man who believes he's entitled to reconstruct Yokolam's mother's face with his hand when she doesn't perform a first wife's duties, as he prescribes them. A man who always has the last word.

I sit at his wooden desk, four feet from his bed, my feet giving way under the weight of his words. I realise all of a sudden how small his room is. On his desk is a high stack of law textbooks, and on the floor several tea-stained mugs. He sits on his bed and pages through a book aimlessly. Between us a silence of separation.

My mind drifts to Nyakale. I wonder what she would think of all this. Whether she and Yokolam would get along. I think of Yokolam's siblings and the years of silence that lie between them. Of nothing said. Of assumptions that have resulted in walls of anger that now seem too high to climb or demolish. Sort of like Nyakale and me. Today I long for my twin sister.

Yokolam and I are sitting on an Akamba bus travelling from Kampala to Jinja. His mother has been hospitalised in Jinja Regional Hospital because of the Army Man. On the streets of Kampala, with no room for even air between the cars, the traffic is moving at the speed of a tortoise. The boda-bodas buzz between the cars, passengers holding on for their lives. The sun is at its peak, you can tell by the sweat particles dripping from foreheads. Everyone in a hurry, minds adrift.

We sit quietly, my hand in his. I wonder what is occupying

his mind; but with time, I've learnt there are moments when I must just leave him to his thoughts.

I wonder why Yokolam's mother stays with the Army Man. Why, after all these years, hospitals and bruises, she has not left. I know here there are things expected of a woman, and that's fine – but not turning a blind eye to your own injuries. That's not something that falls under a woman's duty to her husband. When I bring this up with Mama her response is, "The affairs of another home are not ours to question."

My eyelids heavy, I can feel myself drifting from consciousness as I fall asleep on Yokolam's shoulder.

When I open my eyes, the sun is going to the source of the Nile, to set just beyond it. It's early evening when we arrive in Jinja. We get off the bus and wait for a boda-boda to take us from the bus stop to the hospital. The roads here are dusty. I'm glad I am wearing my dark navy jeans and a black top, with a kitenge wrapped around my head so the dust does not spoil my hair.

The hospital is understaffed and underdeveloped. The nurses and doctors move their bodies out of habit, but they would rather be anywhere else. "Hello, how are you?" we greet a nurse, and she replies, "We are well." It's a routine answer to a routine question. Her truthful response would probably be the polar opposite.

There are no visiting hours at the hospital per se. Yokolam asks which ward his mother is in and we follow the nurse down crowded passages, side-stepping the patients lying on the floor on mats and kitenges, to his mother's bed.

The bruises change her, and not only in the marks they leave on her face. She seems like a woman who has crept further inward. There's a drip attached to her arm and black-blue bruises from her wrist to her upper arm. A white bandage covers her left eye. Given the nature of things, she's not among the worst cases here, so the doctors are hoping we'll take her home today to make room for more critical patients.

Yokolam can't look at her. It's as though looking stings his eyes. Anyone else would assume he's never seen her like this before. He blinks uncontrollably as tears gather – but he won't cry, not in front of his mother. He keeps the tears relentlessly at bay. Her only son, he must be strong for her.

For as long as I've known him, he's told me stories of all the nights; with his adolescent understanding, he'd attempt to nurse her back to health. He'd bandage her wounds, fish from dusk to dawn to make sufficient money to go to the centre and buy her pain medication. We've seen her like this before, and I know growing up he's seen it countless times more. There's fear in his eyes. I stroke his shoulder, knowing how inadequate this gesture is. Anger wells in my chest like a fire.

We organise a van that will transport Mama, Yokolam and me back to the village. The story makes its rounds in whispers between neighbours. Everyone knows that Yokolam's mama's disappearance, and return in bandages, is the doing of the Army Man, but no one will intervene in another man's affairs.

He's there when we enter the house. Yokolam does not speak to him, not even a hello.

The Army Man looks shocked to see his first wife. "Oh God, what has happened to this wife of mine, oh God, why me?" he cries, raising his massive hands to cover his face. His shirt incorrectly buttoned, too-long, dirty trousers folded above his ankles. His towering body looks unsuited to distress; although he's aged, he's still as strong as a young soldier.

There's what seems to be genuine sadness in his voice, and his eyes fill with tears. I can't understand this, how a man can be confused by the actions of his very own hands. As he puts on this show, Yokolam's mother nods and smiles a sympathetic smile. I wonder who her sympathy is for.

"Janet, come here immediately!" he shouts.

She's his third wife – well, wife-to-be, as the ceremonies are yet to happen. He speaks to her as though she's a soldier and he's her lieutenant. In the distance, you see Janet abandoning what she's doing to come running.

"Yes, Sir!" she says, adding to the theatrics.

"You better make sure Mama Yokolam is fed sufficiently, three times a day, you hear? And now you take her from this boy and put her to rest in the main house." He sounds almost proud.

"Of course, Sir."

The younger woman approaches us. Gently taking Yokolam's mama from his arms, allowing her to lean against her shoulder for support.

"I love you, Mama," Yokolam whispers as his mother is led away, tears again collecting in his eyes.

Yokolam and I walk up to the mountain, site of our sweetest childhood memories. Next to me is a man who is broken – by his defiant love for his mother, and equally by the hate for the Army Man festering in his heart. I see it also in the way he's given me so much, too much – worlds of his time and attention: all things he considers the best of him, the things his father never gave. As we walk in silence, from the corner of my eye I catch him staring at me. I know that look. It's a look that hopes to be better, do better; to love me in ways he's still finding out are possible.

"I love who you are," I say, reaching out to hold his hand.

"I promise, Achen, I promise to be better than him." An all-consuming determination causes his voice to quiver.

When we get to the top of the mountain, the sun has long set. We sit and look up at the sky, filled with innumerable scattered stars. This is one of the simple things that remind me that I'm home.

"This is why the village wins. This alone," I say playfully.

He smiles faintly, his head on my lap, and closes his eyes.

We listen to sounds of laughter echoing from a nearby village. Night time is when the mzees meet for the drinking of waragi and the exchange of stories, children lying at their feet. We sit in silence for a while.

"I don't know what to do. She won't leave him and come live in a small apartment in Kampala. Ah, why doesn't she see that this devotion she has to this man will kill her? I am helpless, Achen. How can she not see?"

"The thing is, Yokolam, love is a strange thing. It's a thing that can make us hate ourselves for the good of someone else. It has the ability to change us, and that's only understood by the people who are in love." I know this isn't what he wants to hear, but it's what needs to be said. We can't control everything.

Now we're sitting leaning against each other.

"Achen, remember when we were children, dashing up the mountain? We'd spread our arms and pretend we were birds. I wish we were birds right now and that we could fly away, far away."

"Of course I remember, how could I not? That changed everything," I giggle, remembering how I was always so impressed by Yokolam. A boy knowledgeable and concerned about the world.

"Achen, one day we'll have to leave Uganda and search for other things. I can't leave without you, so promise at least that you will think about it."

"But you know where I stand, Yokolam. Not even love can cause me to leave here. I can't lie to you and say that I'll think about it. For me, there is nothing to think about."

Again, we sit in silence; you can hear insects in the bushes. There are fireflies lighting up and then disappearing just as fast. The moon is full, and its light makes us not feel how late it's actually become.

I think of Jaja and Papa's love story, one of the most beautiful things, although old age has taken their lives. Theirs is a love that has been engrained in all my memories. Papa was injured when government soldiers came hunting those who supported the opposition party. Papa lost one of his legs then, and couldn't do much for himself. The leg was cut off by the doctors, and he was given a wooden stick to find a way to balance his body. Jaja showed Papa a devotion that I'd never seen before. Hers was a love that was selfless and giving. I think this is why Jaja died at eighty-three years, still as strong as an ox. Their story is part of why I feel it's a greater honour to be of service than to be served: the former enlarges you.

The problem with sitting on the mountain is that we lose track of time. As we approach the compound, we're welcomed by silence. Everything is still, everyone asleep, with auras of dreams filling the air and fatigue lifting from people's bodies.

We stand outside for a bit, the weather warm as always. The sky's now a bit darker, but warmth caresses our skin like it does here and nowhere else. Yokolam looks up and starts telling me irrelevant facts about astronomy. The spark in his eyes when he explains such things – I wish I could keep it in a bottle for dark nights. To remind him that this is who he is. I've heard it before, but each time I widen my eyes and smile, because I know tonight of all nights, he needs this.

"Showoff," I say, laughing.

In this moment, I want to freeze time, so that for a little bit longer it's just the two of us here. Not weighed down by things we cannot change, by things we see differently.

"I must go and sleep," I say eventually, wishing my legs were not so tired. Otherwise, I would have preferred to just be here, standing with him.

"Ah, come on, just stay a little longer," he says, reaching to hug me.

He holds me closely. I feel his heart beating fast, but as we stay in each other's arms, his heart rate slows, excitement giving way to comfort. I realise how strong and tall he has become.

"Goodnight, the one I love," he confidently declares into the air.

"Goodnight."

I walk towards the main house where his mama is lying. I know he's still standing there, waiting for me to go inside. Although the village is small and everyone knows everyone, he insists on ensuring I'm safe before he can go in and rest. As I reach for the door, I look back at him, touch my heart and point to the mountain. He does the same, then walks to the adjacent hut where he sleeps when he's home, sharing the space with some of his cousins.

There's a thin mattress in the room where Yokolam's mama is sleeping. I'm not used to seeing her look so peaceful, and it reassures me. I grab a mat and kitenge to cover myself. I'm thinking of today, of my love for Yokolam and his love for his family.

Just as my thoughts are subsiding and sleep slowly begins to cover me, I hear a sound right outside. At first I can't make out what it is: it sounds like the cries of a bull when it's being cruelly jabbed and taunted; but I can tell that these cries are those of a person, wailing and screaming from the depths of their stomach, in anguish.

I go outside and the first thing I smell is a fire. Sitting in front of it is the Army Man. He is weeping and placing his hands in the fire, and not in the playful, daring way we did as kids. Instead, his entire hand is in the fire. I'm not sure whether the intensity of his screams is because of the internal or external anguish.

"What have I done? What have these hands done to my wife? These hands do not deserve to live, so I will punish them!"

Then once again he places them in the furnace. I'm standing in plain sight, but somehow he does not see me. He looks like he's in a trance.

How can this can be? Has guilt has taken over his body?

This is not the Army Man. I'm convinced I am dreaming.

I am not dreaming. This is the Army Man.

AMBER

Amber is not one colour but many, borrowing shades of yellow, orange, brown and red. It is the closest colour to fire, and like fire it is transitory. When you find that thing that sets your soul on fire, you can't help but run towards it, fear in one hand and courage in the other.

Nyakale

The thing with a fire is that it doesn't tell you here, look, I am approaching. It comes like a thief at night, silent – and the next minute it's all around you, consuming all things in its path.

It's the beginning of our last year, full of the excitement of finality. We've outgrown the thrill of independence that came with starting university, and now desire an even greater freedom. The curtains have closed on the years of rehearsal; the real opening night is imminent. Of course, we're delighted this is what all those exams we wrote in the Sports Centre lead to: the right of passage that is the graduation ceremony in Jameson Hall. Jammie Hall stands at the centre of campus, embodying the dreams and desires of multitudes of students. The dreams of parents, of aunts and uncles, of entire communities holding their breaths to finally ululate in pride;

to call out the names, and names of forefathers; to recognise the progression of a generation.

I've been trying to call Lwazi for some time now, but his phone keeps going to voicemail; when it's not off, it just rings continuously. The last time we spoke, yes, I was mad. At him. At us. With how, over time, he'd developed an indifference to my concerns, like they weren't real. He couldn't hide it: it was in his weary eyes, his lips set in a straight line, his distant body language. Indifferent when I tried to explain why this was a big deal. Indifferent to our conversations, which he once thought were riveting. The pendulum of our conversations swung between arguments and indifference – before the transition to radio silence.

It was the intimacy that tore us apart. The expectations that come with being known. Knowledge is the thing that sets love on fire – and can burn it down. The things I knew he once was, he was no longer. It was this I could not stomach.

I walk to the engineering building to meet Mufasa for coffee. Campus seems a lot more congested than usual. People are clustering in groups, pointing at cellphone screens. There's laughter and a sense of shock.

"Nyakale, you will not believe what just happened," Mufasa says, a concoction of emotions on his face – excitement, alarm and urgency.

"Tell me already!"

"Hmmm, how do I say this… have you been on Twitter lately?"

"What's happened now?"

"So, the Rhodes statue, you won't believe this, but apparently human poo was thrown on it!"

"What? Why?"

"Madness, right? But apparently, the statue's a symbol of South Africa's colonial past and the oppression of black people. It's a protest."

The last sentence takes a while for me to digest. I feel a sudden excitement in the pit of my stomach – a thrill. Is it the danger of such a thing, or the sleeping giant of questioning it awakes?

"When? How? Who? What happens now?" A million thoughts are running through my mind.

"I don't know, Kale. But I imagine it will not go unnoticed."

"Which is the intention, I'd assume."

Walking down to lower campus, I think about this conversation with Mufasa, and about the time I have left until the end of varsity. There's pressure to decide what I want to do with the rest of my life – right now, I have no idea. All I know is I don't want to settle for the easiest path. I want something more.

I'm walking down the stairs, totally submerged in my thoughts, oblivious to my surroundings, when a slight stench circles my nostrils. I can't see the faeces, but the smell confirms that what Mufasa related has indeed happened. Rhodes is seated on his throne, leaning forward with his right leg slightly elevated, chin resting on his right hand and elbow on his knee. Looking into the distance, the expression on his face at first glance is one of indifference.

I wonder what was going through the guy's mind when he threw the faeces. What had he seen when he looked at this statue, and why hadn't I seen it? What was it in him, and why had the rest of us been oblivious for all this time? I want to know more. I'm alight with curiosity for his thoughts, but also the thoughts going through everyone else's minds.

Something makes me want to talk to Lwazi and hear what he thinks. I send him a text but he doesn't respond. So instead I grab my journal and start documenting the questions spinning in my head.

There's something about this movement that I know I can't separate myself from. It's not only what's happening on campus that intrigues me. It's the numerous voices in the media: so many people freely offering opinions – authoritative, cutting like a blade through the movement and declaring it medium-rare. Others juggling multiple unfounded theories, trying to form conclusions. It's this urge to simplify complex matters that Lwazi and I both hated. I know what I want to do. I call Mufasa.

"Kale, sorry I haven't called in a while, things have been extraordinarily busy."

"There's something I've been meaning to ask you," I begin. I'm a bit concerned about what he'll think of my decision; whatever it is, his opinion will matter to me.

"I don't know if you've been following Rhodes Must Fall, but I've been thinking. I may be considering, possibly, joining the Varsity news team, if they'll let me help cover the story. I know your friend Boitumelo works there… I was wondering if she'd be open to that?"

"Nyakale, why would you want to do that? I mean, it's our final year of university, it shouldn't concern you – and, well, it's not like you entirely relate to the movement and what it stands for."

"Mufasa, I'm choosing to ignore your last sentence. Listen, this is something I need to do. It's important."

"I honestly don't think you should – you don't have the luxury of time to waste, with final year Economics Honours. But if you insist, fine. I'll give Boity a call and let you know what she says."

"Thank you, Mufasa. I need this."

I'm sitting in what we've started calling Azania House. There's an energy in the room – the coming together of a deep-seated need to know, frustration, all the pain that's been endured, and enquiring minds. I sit in the front row with a pen and paper, ferociously writing down every detail of what I see around me. Boity's promised to include my article if she finds it suitable. This is enough to ignite what I've discovered to be a passion in me to tell stories. Francine's also been here the whole week, poised as ever, listening intensely, watching and taking notes. I wish I could read her musings.

The facilitators introduce the speaker for today's meeting: a professor who's visiting the campus from the United States, Dr Se-laisse. She's originally from Ghana, but has spent most of her life in the US – she was at Harvard with Francine, and they're old friends. She speaks eloquently, saying not only the things we want to hear, but also some things we're unprepared for. She talks about how we've come to an intersection of history. About the importance of academic enquiry in understanding who we are, where we come from and our place in the world.

"There's something about knowing that haunts us, but my faith has me subscribing to the idea that the truth sets us free. We can only build once we know and know very well. So, I encourage you all at this time of enquiry to read widely. Not only on racial relations but on the continent and its history… and in your quest, don't forget that being humane is part of our heritage."

At this last line, there are shouts of protest. People are tired, agitated at waiting in the wings for things to unfold.

The professor concludes with stories of her diaspora experience – of growing up in America, the battles of identity she's waged. Songs erupt in the room. In unison, the voices weave together a melody that is more than just song and words.

Then the unfathomable begins, as one by one people stand up and tell their stories. Stories of what blackness has meant throughout their lives, stories of where they come from, stories of feeling isolated because of their economic standing.

I'm slightly shocked to see Ntombi stand.

She tells us about how her private-school education and privilege has created a hedge of separation that makes her feel like she doesn't belong. She isn't white, although she closely conforms to the white lifestyle. She isn't black, because she doesn't share the common black-child narrative.

I spot Lwazi at the front with some of the student leaders. I catch his gaze, and we stare deeply into each other's eyes. Remembering our passionate, politically infused conversations. Now here he is, seated in the front, and I'm jotting down notes and taking pictures. Both of us where we should be.

A guy in a faded red T-shirt stands up to speak. "I remember being in first year. It was orientation week, which meant there were activities on campus every other day. I'd slip away when all my friends were lining up to get on the bus to transport us to the next activity. I'd go while everyone was talking. I'm sure they thought I went to the bathroom. But I went to my room, because I knew I didn't have the money to pay for the activity. I'm the son of a domestic worker. My mother gave me all the money she had before I left, but it wasn't much – I have two younger siblings that she needed to think about. My mother doesn't know this world, and my father left long ago. My varsity career has been a time of shape-shifting, trying to fit in, in a world that no one equipped me for."

The room briefly falls silent, before singing erupts once again.

The last conversation I had with Uncle, he told me to stop chasing the wind and focus on my education, the thing he sent me to university for. I wish he could see all the learning that's happening, the things that lectures fall short of teaching. I see it in the faces around me: people need to know where they come from; they need to express their fears, to find their places in the world. I want to stand up and share my story too, but I feel unqualified.

I'm in my flat, in front of my laptop, fifteen minutes before my scheduled call with Aisha. I'm rampaging through civil rights and black consciousness literature, but I can't stop thinking about that guy, the one with the dreadlocks hanging to his shoulders and the red T-shirt. How he'd stood up and silently climbed on one of the desks. Azania House filled to capacity.

I'd been watching him before the meeting started. Everyone was sitting in groups, caught up in conversation. I was sitting alone, as Mufasa had an exam to prepare for and Nina also had somewhere to be. I noticed him, also alone, on the floor with his back against the wall, his shoulders slanting downward. He kept turning, twisting, tapping his foot, shaking his head. He tried to speak but his words were whispers.

"Stuck. I'm stuck here." He exhaled loudly. "I need this degree – but I can't breathe here. It's suffocating, this dance of social class. I am so exhausted…"

His words struck me. I wondered if anyone else had heard him, but it didn't seem so.

The Skype ringtone interrupts my thoughts.

"Aisha! I finally know. I think I understand why you had to study medicine. It all makes sense. It's this sense of a greater purpose that transcends selfishness."

"Wait, Nyakale, what in the world are you talking about?"

"Okay so journalism, that's what I want to do next year. With everything happening on campus, it's become clear that this is what excites me. It's this compulsive interest in the fates of others. In sitting, listening and interviewing people. In wondering what happens in their minds. I need to understand, Aisha."

"I know, Nyakale. Sometimes we take leaps of faith, and they teach us understanding. I get it. Medicine is a lot like that for me. These aren't just patients. They are people's loved ones. There are people at home waiting for them to return. I get it. I am so excited for you."

"Thank you. I needed you to get it."

The following weeks are filled with even more media coverage and debate about what the protests all mean.

Then the day we've all been waiting for arrives. Management has decided: Rhodes will fall. It's exactly a month after the protests began – 9 April 2015. A red truck with a hoist arrives on the campus. There are thousands of students and lecturers gathered around the statue. A sea of smart phones in the air waiting to capture the historical moment. Once the forklift is in place, the crowd starts to count down: "Three... two... one...!"

Rhodes is removed from where he'd been seated. A section of the crowd erupts into song, elated: "Umoya wami uyavuma."

It's time to wrap up the new edition of Varsity, covering everything that's happened over the past few months. I'm struggling with my article: how do you begin to depict a subject as complex as this? There's so much to say, and I fear condensing it will make it lose its value.

What the protests did was expose the things in all of us that we thought we had a handle on. Suddenly, our speech was no longer politically correct. We had to abandon the notion that our common humanity bonded us together. The extent of our differences was on display for all to see; we found that we lived galaxies apart, although we walked side by side on campus.

I sit in my room and read my article over and over. It's terrible and comes nowhere near the piece I should have written. But I understand why I had to write it. It was to teach me empathy. I know why people avoid empathy. Empathy is exhausting – entering another's reality, one you know nothing about, why would anyone choose to do that?

Then it dawns on me – this isn't really about the statue. The statue, as it was when erected, is a symbol that brings people together around a cause. The cause of transformation, of creating safe spaces. I think about how university is a collage, the intersection of different lived and living experiences. We are all equal in our quest for knowledge, but the weights we carry on our shoulders differ, oh so significantly.

I know now what I'll end my article with:

> The nodding heads in Azania House expressed a shared truth; and so did the boycotting of these

meetings, the labelling of them as stupid. We're all made from the places we've been, the people we've encountered and the moments we've lived through. This makes all the difference in how we see the world.

Graduation has come and gone. I stand on Jammie Steps and look at the lights below, scattered everywhere on the darkness like stars. Dying stars, perhaps. There's something about this last year that has got inside of me, leaving this undeniable feeling that things will never be the same. Lwazi and I sat on Jammie stairs countless times together, dreaming about the years after university, about our families and the places we call home. It's a funny thing, when a person you thought you knew like the back of your own hand becomes a stranger. Strangers, friends, lovers, strangers, we'd gone the whole three hundred and sixty degrees.

On my way down to middle campus, rugby fields on either side, I turn back for one last look at the past four years. I gaze up at the grand buildings of the great University of Cape Town, feeling far removed from them. For the first time, this view leaves me wanting more. The exact opposite of the feeling that morning when Aunty Mercy pushed open the door to my room, shouting, "We thank God!" In her hands my acceptance letter to the University of Cape Town. My heart cartwheeling.

Aunty's fears for me are quenched by how proud she is; I can do no wrong in her eyes. It has upset Uncle, though: my newfound interest in politics, all my questions.

But I know that I've found the thing that I'm going to do for as long as I'm on this earth. I no longer simply see bank tellers, gardeners, businessmen or artists: I want to know the back stories. The things that make them wake up every morning, or upset them. This desire consumes me. Even inanimate objects have become living, breathing things, with their own stories – who designed that table? Where did they get the wood? The thrill starts slowly; initially I can't decipher what it is about the stories that compels me. It's not writing them so much as sitting cross-legged, asking questions. Finding the puzzle pieces. Interviewing people and listening intently for the things they don't say. Then asking the right questions to reveal what they actually want to say.

My heart also knows now that I need to go back to Uganda. I can finally articulate this deeply embedded desire. It's not the economics of poverty that I want to explore, although this topic is dear to me, but rather the stories that live there and that I need to uncover.

"But Aunty Mercy, I can't explain it any clearer. I'm just certain that I must go. I need to go home." Home? I quickly correct myself: "To Uganda."

"Nyakale, you know things are tough there. Ah, visiting isn't a problem, but this idea of yours of staying in Kampala indefinitely – for what? My husband, talk to this daughter of ours!" Aunty Mercy looks at me wearily. I can't help but feel that every wrinkle pressed into her forehead is my fault. She frowns, clapping her hands together then raising them up, declaring defeat.

Uncle is straight-backed at the wooden kitchen table. He looks up from his open newspaper to face me, the wayward daughter. I shift my weight from one foot to the other, trying to remain composed. "Mercy, this one will make us talk until we turn blue. It's been months, trying to convince her otherwise. With her few years on earth, it seems she knows better than us. The tickets are booked, what can we do?"

"My concern is this journalism interest that Nyakale has developed – what African child becomes a journalist?" Uncle exclaims, looking around the room for an answer.

Uncle reads the paper daily; it isn't that he hasn't come across innumerable African journalists. What he means to say is it's fine for other people's children, but not his own.

"Okay," I say, almost losing my self control, "then tell me what African children become?"

I know the answer to my question – doctor, accountant. But today I'm tired of marching on command, of never saying what I mean but rather what's expected of me.

Uncle's eyes look like they're about to fall out of their sockets. "Respect, Nyakale!" he thunders. "Do not forget who raised you, and the values you were raised with. African children become something respectable. Do you hear me?"

But I know that he too has decided to wave his white flag in surrender, like Aunty Mercy's raised arms. The space between us feels wider and more vacant than ever before. It's just me, I think, and not in a liberating sense. I am alone here.

The stories I find in Uganda will heal the voids within me. I feel it. I long to understand this other piece of me: what the country is like. What my mother is like. I want to forgive her. A piece of me hopes that when I see her it will be like a scene out of the movies, where all my resentment is overwhelmed by joy. And Achen and I, we will be best friends.

Tomorrow, it will be our twenty-second birthday.

Achen

I'm at Nilo's internet café again, because the reception's better here. I haven't heard from Yokolam in a while. His phone defaults to voicemail, but with no message, just that beeping sound. When I eventually get hold of him, he sounds aloof, with a lot of I's and me's in his vocabulary. He no longer seems concerned about his mother, asking carelessly, "Is she still choosing to suffer with that madman?" When I ask why he hasn't answered my calls, he mechanically recites excuses: "This stupid phone of mine and its battery" or, "Ah, you know, these lecturers are merciless. I've been studying with no time at all to even sleep, imagine!"

Something about him has changed, and my perception of

him has changed, too. I've gradually become intolerant of his ideas of law and justice. His definition of justice feels far removed from the realities of those he vowed to help. It sounds like he enjoys the language of justice more than its reality. Action. This is what we need, not language. Uganda has enough spokesmen.

"Yokolam, can you hear me?"

"Achen, is that you?"

An idiotic question, because I'm calling him on my phone. "Yes, it's me. I'm calling to check if you're even alive?"

"I am alive. It's just, the workload has been crazy. Some of the students have taken to this senseless striking business, it's crazy. The campus has been closed for two weeks, but do you think the lecturers will care? No, they won't, we'll just be bombarded by even more difficult tests. It's crazy."

"It's crazy" – an expression he must have learnt lately and decided to overuse.

Twenty minutes of listening to Yokolam talk and talk about his life, his thoughts, without a second to spare to ask me how I am.

I want to give him an update on the Women's Cooperative and the amount of support we have. The word's spreading, and I want to share the excitement that's bubbling in my belly. But I know that any response he gives will be more disappointing than his silence. I long for Cynthia and Sandra, to share this moment with the two people who'd understand entirely what this means to me, despite their playful mockery.

And I miss Nafula every day. Days like this just make it harder.

The story has made its rounds: variations on how it was the beauty that God gave her that led her astray. We know she's in Kampala. One of the neighbours came to tell Aunty Anna that they saw her in Lumumba Avenue: "She was standing there naked!" A way of saying she was flimsily dressed.

I blame myself. How did I miss her restlessness? How didn't I see that, with age, her desire for "more" would only grow?

Sadly, I pick up my phone and begin scrolling through old pictures. Of me and Nafula. Of me and Yokolam. I wish I could bring back the boy of my memories, but I'm afraid he's long gone.

Cynthia's promised to initiate a three-way call. I can't help staring eagerly at the clock as it inches towards three. Cynthia, as expected, calls ten minutes late.

"Hi!", "Hello!", "Ladies!" – our words frantically colliding.

"My girls, what's the latest?" Cynthia begins, upbeat. "Ache, are you still trying to overthrow the government?"

Sandra and I both burst into warm laughter. Cynthia hasn't changed a bit.

"Yes, I am. We've had five meetings in the villages, each drawing thirty-plus women. We're actually planning a mass march in Kampala in about a month. It's unreal – the women from the Ugandan Women's Network called to ask whether I'd like to partner with them. And this organisation called Speak, "Women with a Voice", and a lot of independent activists – they've all got in touch with me, looking to cover the story. I have to pinch myself to know I'm not dreaming."

"We're so proud of you," the two say in unison.

"Sandra, how are things down South?"

"Things are going fine, you know how it is."

Cynthia and I immediately recognise the evasion of those words. It's been tough for Sandra: not only the adjustment to South Africa and uni, but having to supplement her scholarship by working after class.

"Guys, I am suffering! The weather in the UK, it's terrible. How do people here survive is a question I ask every day. It's cold, dark and wet. I haven't seen the sun in almost two weeks, imagine! I'm sure the rash on my face is because of a dire lack of vitamin D."

We laugh – we know Cynthia's exaggerating to avoid admitting that she's actually enjoying it there. Then I grow serious: "I don't know if you two have heard, but things have been bad in the village. It still hasn't rained. Come next week, it'll be a full nine months... it's been better for us, with Aunt Mercy sending money, but some families are really starving. A woman came to the compound the other day asking for help – her children had gone to bed without food for two days in a row."

"What a terrible thing, I can't believe Mama didn't call to tell me." Sandra's voice is distressed.

"She probably didn't want you to worry. There's not much anyone can do. We just have to wait on the rain."

All the people's actions in the village are now influenced by the drought. Any joy has been silenced by the groans of hunger and supplication. Mama is cautious as she cleans the catfish, ensuring that no good piece is wasted by the knife cutting too deep, her hand lightly exerting only the required strength. I can tell that the years of mourning have taken their toll on her. She walks a little slower these days, and her figure is shrunken. Kintu has taken to joining the fishermen on the Nile, so he only returns now and then, but always with a lot of fish. Mama dances whenever she sees him in the distance. He runs towards her, fish in a kavera and arms stretched out. He's taller and stronger, each time he comes home.

And Nafula has lost herself in the city, a thing no one mentions. Aunty Juliet pretends this hasn't happened, adamantly veering far away from any talk about it. She will not have it. Since the elders don't talk, I too eat my words.

I can see the strain in the measured portions served, in the children being told to lick their plates clean. The children have taken to eating slowly. Not slowly like we used to do as children, savouring the flavours and making whoever finished first jealous. It's not a game now; the children eat slowly in the hope that the slower they eat, the fuller their stomachs will become.

It's the day before the big march. Sinai has called to confirm that we'll commence the march from Parliament Avenue and end in Ntinda, where most of the wealthy politicians and retirees live.

Sinai is an activist based in Kampala. She graduated with distinction from Makerere, but with jobs hard to come by, she's taken to activism and blogging. She has this surety of self that makes you feel confident too. She articulates each word clearly, with conviction in her voice, and makes you want to stand in agreement. I haven't met her in person, but I imagine she has a fine, upright posture. A woman who speaks this confidently has to be beautiful.

I'm awake earlier than usual, unable to keep the excitement and fear welling within me at bay. I sit outside, running through the programme for the day in my head. We'll assemble on Parliament Avenue. I'll address the crowd, together with Sinai. I haven't managed to string words together over the past couple of days, but I'm sure words will come to me when I need them.

I go inside to collect some clothes from the drawer. Kintu wanders into my hut, a pleased smile on his face and his hands behind his back.

"What do you have there? Come on, show me."

He slowly reveals his right hand, his left still behind his back. Then after keeping me in suspense, he finally pulls out from behind him a breathtaking sculpture of a woman. One leg is set forward and slightly bent at the knee, like she's walking towards something. I love it.

"Thank you so much, Kintu." I hug him tightly, his forearms on my back and his hands tightly holding my shoulders. As I pull away, his eyes are downcast. How I will miss him, although I'll only be away for a few weeks.

"Achen, I can't believe you've decided to go and kill yourself in Kampala. I have already lost one child and you insist on leaving me childless." Mama's voice is cold and her words sharp. She's outside on a small wooden stool, cleaning the fish. "Why must you be so stubborn? Have you heard what happens to groups who protest in Kampala, have you? They get beaten and thrown into prison, without achieving anything."

I stand silently, knowing that she still has things she wishes to say.

"If you want to change things, you stay here. Look at those crops withering!" She points. "Achen, people are starving. This land rights business is pointless – there's no life in this land. If it doesn't rain, even if women own the land it will still be worthless." Mama says these words like she's relaying simple facts. "I don't know how long the stored crops will last us. I know I should keep them for us only, but how can I watch my neighbour starve? How can I withhold the good I can give them today for a tomorrow that is not promised to any of us?"

"Mama, this is something I have to do for myself. I'm sorry that you don't understand why, but I have to. I promise I will be back in one piece." My words are solemn. I look at the sky, willing my tears not to fall. The sky is a bright blue, no clouds in sight.

We meet at the centre, where four matatus are waiting for us. Women standing in huddles, sharing tales. When it's time to leave, I sit in the front seat of the matatu leading the convoy. There are twenty-plus women in each vehicle. The women with me are the younger members of the movement, and the back of our matatu is a stew of enthusiasm and eagerness to get to Kampala.

Two hours into the journey, chatter is replaced by the soft sound of sleep. The few who are awake talk in hushed tones. I look out the window at the green fields. I hope that Mama's wrong, and that I'm not wasting all these women's time, dangling false hope in front of them. I close my eyes and recall the words of one of the eldest members of our group: "Wisdom is wealth, my child, the wealth of one's life. You need to trust yourself more, Achen. You will somehow always know what to do."

Her words subdue the fear lurking in my heart. I sleep.

When I smell Kampala, I slowly open my eyes. Cars bumper to bumper, moving at a snail's pace, with fumes lifting from their engines. Travelling the next fifty kilometres will probably take another hour. The streets are filled with people, distracted, all in a hurry. Manoeuvring through the traffic are hawkers, all competing to sell the same variety of things: fried bananas, sodas, chicken pieces and chapati.

We finally pull into Parliament Avenue, where the streets are flooded with women. Old women, young women, short and tall women. Some already have their placards in hand, using them to shelter from the sun.

"We are also citizens of the country."

"Respect WOMEN's rights."

I see a girl vigorously waving in the distance. That must be Sinai. She is, as I had imagined, beautiful. She has a green and yellow kitenge wrapped on her head and is otherwise dressed all in black. Her aura of certainty is even more tangible in person.

"Are you ready, Achen?" In her voice, the familiarity that camaraderie breeds.

"I think I am."

I stand in front of this crowd of women, wondering what words of significance I can say to spur them on. Sinai comes to stand next to me, and I immediately feel myself steadying.

"Sarah Nyendwoha Ntiro, the first woman in East and Central Africa to graduate with a university degree," I begin. "A daughter of a teacher; one of the first six women to join Makerere when it started accepting women. She refused to be paid when she became a lecturer, when she found out that she was getting paid less than her male colleagues. Now look at the number of women in universities across Uganda. It started with one woman – and today, we are the women who will continue the fight. Today, let us remember that this march is for us but also for the generations to come."

"We are the BUILDERS of this society!" Sinai shouts, in a voice that seems too loud for her slim frame.

We march hand in hand, singing and chanting, until we reached Ntinda. There we stand defiantly, calling on the government to replace the customary law and ensure that women in the villages can own land.

Before we know it, a cloud of terror engulfs us – police and army vehicles approaching from every direction. Women desperately running, trying to disperse before the police begin with the rubber bullets. Some are screaming at the top of their lungs, trying to fight off the police who are overpowering them.

I want to shrink back but I can't. Sinai and I shout even louder: "Women are citizens too!"

The police grab at us viciously, tears of passion and terror flowing down our faces. I know that Mama will hear about this by tomorrow morning, which makes me cry more. Our bodies are pulled, dragged and beaten. We're thrown in the back of a police van, and the police threaten to detain us in Luzira Prison, a few kilometres from Kampala city centre. I begin to plead, as Sinai remains defiant.

Eventually, the three policemen who are holding us walk away to discuss the matter among themselves. The larger man in the trio approaches the vehicle, unlocks the door and lets us out.

"You two, you're free to go – but next time you won't be so lucky."

"Yes sir," I say quickly.

Sinai just walks past him, unaffected.

In the distance lies the collateral damage: women's blood staining the tar and sand. My body feels paralysed, my mind racing through a million thoughts:

Was this the right thing to do?

Will anything good come of this?

What if nothing comes of this?

There are journalists now on the scene, taking pictures and

talking to some of the women. As I slowly return to my body, Sinai still stands beside me.

"It would've only been for one night," she says.

I realise the experience of being detained isn't new to her. She holds my hand as we walk back to the women and find a place to sit with them. And I understand that this is true strength: not spectacular, not dramatic, but real.

Mama holds me tight, relief overshadowing her anger. She doesn't speak about the march, although I know she's heard about it. She hugs me, her tears dampening my top.

"My daughter. My daughter!" she cries, unmindful of our neighbours.

"I love you Mama. I am sorry."

My words elicit deeper sobs from her trembling body.

Later, I go to the centre and buy all the newspapers that covered the story. I read the features over and over, wishing to relive the moment, but also relieved that I'm home.

The article mentions both Sinai and me as the "leaders" of the movement. Yokolam has to have seen it, or at least heard of it. I'm running out of sensible excuses for why he hasn't called to check that I'm okay, now of all times. I'm not sure about much, lately, but I know we've been holding on to the love of our youth, to who we once were; it's time we both accepted we're no longer those people. Yokolam and I need to let each other go. We'll both be better for it. He doesn't understand my activism and I don't understand his law, and because these are things that now make us ourselves, we no longer understand each other. Something changed on 8 March: our demonstration has shaken me to my core, but also unlocked a renewed sense of wonder.

Cynthia heard the news through Facebook, and sent me a message: "I am proud of you but also sorry that those police would do that to you. You will find that the police are the same in other countries, always exercising their power on civilians. Thinking of you – and I'll see you on your birthday! C."

Her words give me comfort.

The drought has not improved. I look into the store hut: a dried mud floor, a grass-thatched roof, but no grain or vegetables. I fall to my knees with the dust around me rising like an exhalation, welcoming me to the ground, tears running down my face.

And as my first tear falls into the dust, the rains begin to fall.

AN IMAGE IN A MIRROR

Strange, how humans desire to see themselves in mirror image: staring back from the glass, their parts reversed – but their colours reflected.

So here I am. Staring out of an aeroplane window down onto a strange, dry landscape. My mother's letter burns in my pocket. What the hell am I thinking?

"Welcome to Entebbe International Airport," reads the sign, striped with the red, black and yellow of the Ugandan flag. I walk under it, through a broken automatic door that stands permanently open. The three-storey building looks minute and run-down compared to OR Tambo International. I collect my luggage and take the only exit. Outside, crowds of people are seated on benches, and taxi drivers huddle by the door, calling "Madam!" and "Sir!" to grab the attention of passers-by. The heat is all consuming.

I'm startled by a tap on my shoulder: "Nyakale!"

This must be my Aunt Juliet, the last-born of my aunts. She looks slightly like Aunty Mercy, but tall, with long, elegant arms. Her hair is wrapped in green-and-blue-patterned material, matching the kitenge around her waist. She's wearing flip-flops, and dust has gathered on her long feet.

"I hope your mother told you that I'd be fetching you? Ah, but you and Achen – if I didn't know better, I'd have thought you were her!" she declares joyfully, reaching to hold my face between her hands.

Your mother – for a moment I wonder who she's referring to, Aunty Mercy or the woman who gave birth to me.

"Aunty! I'm so glad you spotted me! It slipped my mind to ask Aunty Mercy, I mean my mother, for your number," I clumsily explain.

"Don't worry, my dear, just hand me your bags." My luggage is already halfway out of my hands and into hers. "It's too dark to travel now, so we'll spend the night in Kampala, and early in the morning we will leave for the village, my dear. You know, at my age, I can't even see the road properly at night," she laughs.

She keeps glancing at me, smiling. At least she seems happy to see me. We make our way to the car. I'm struggling to control my wandering eyes and pay attention to Aunt Juliet. I'm exhausted, but also excited: everything is so unfamiliar. There are crowds of people laughing, hugging, chatting loudly in all these new languages that I can't understand. I've never seen so many variations of the gomesi, the floor-length garment, which Aunty Mercy wears for important events. They hold their skirts up slightly as they walk, vibrant colours simmering in the afternoon light.

"How are the people in South Africa?"

"Everyone is doing well, Aunty."

"And school? We hear that you just completed your degree, and very well at that. You are making us all so proud! Nyakale, my sister tells me that you will put the village on the map!"

I laugh awkwardly, having run out of small talk.

In the car, the radio blares in a language foreign to me. Outside, on either side of the narrow road, life is happening. I see people by candlelight, frying food, selling vegetables and chicken. People seated on crates, drinking and laughing. Old women kneeling to arrange their wares on mats – or are they praying?

The traffic is dense, even at this time of night. Taxis pass us, decorated with blue stripes along the sides, the bold declarations on their windshields the only distinguishing feature: "God saves"; "Psalm 23"; "Uganda the Pearl of Africa". A motorbike bravely weaves between the cars, its passenger undisturbed by this recklessness.

The sun rises all at once early in the morning, giving no notice before it slips through the window of my room at the B&B. Wait, is that a cock crowing? I look through the window – Kampala looks like it woke up long before me: the street is busy with traffic and people, the shops are opening up. I get up and shower in cold water, as it's already so warm. Then I sit on the bed, not sure if I should go and knock on Aunt Juliet's door, or go down to breakfast alone. I decide on the former.

I knock cautiously, just in case she's asleep. She opens the door on the third knock. "Good morning daughter, did you sleep well?"

"Very well, thank you. You?"

"I always sleep well, my dear!"

The drive to the village is long; I pass in and out of sleep as Aunt Juliet drives.

Then I open my eyes and all at once realise we are here. This is the moment, the culmination of all my speculation.

It's dry; the heat sears my eyes. The sun follows my every move. I feel lightheaded from the sleep, the heat – and from being here.

Red sand at my feet. Banana trees. Round mud huts with grass-thatched roofs. Many children playing, paying no attention to the heat: tiny bare feet jumping here and there, small bodies covered in dust, all in oversized or tattered clothes. Men sitting in a close circle under a large, magnificent mango tree, drinking through narrow straws from a black clay pot in the centre. The liquid inducing loud laughs and chatter. What I see is life being lived. While Aunt Juliet offloads things from the car, I stand alone, out of place. The stares are excruciating. Are they sneering at me?

A girl is approaching. As she comes closer, I stare in disbelief. We look identical, except she's marginally shorter. I trace the lines of my face in hers – where my eyes are placed, my lips, my hairline. Her skin is smooth. Her eyes seem clearer than my own, bright white, fierce and determined as she walks towards me. Fear creeps into my heart. The girl in front of me is wearing my face.

"Achen." I say the name slowly, each syllable deliberate. I'm hoping that the name sounds right, in my accent. More urgent is the hope that she will like me.

> I can't believe it's her, here in front of me. She's standing there: a tourist. I can tell she's fascinated, her eyes darting around – from the children to the elders and back again. Because those from the city cannot easily comprehend the simple things here. Our lives, her entertainment.
>
> Nyakale's clothes are some of the most beautiful I've seen. A navy dress with white polka dots. Tailor-made, the frills on the sleeves grazing her wrists. A light shade of lipstick on her lips – just enough so you know it's not her natural lip colour. Her hair is beautiful, soft coils styled to fall on either side of the parting. I know she's nervous by the quiver of her bottom lip, but her smile is still lovely. It draws you in. I can tell that she cares very much about the way she looks. Maybe a bit too much. A little too measured, calculated, like something that does not belong here; like she's fragile.
>
> "Good day, Nyakale," I finally say – slowly, like even my mouth is still trying to make sense of things. I knew she was coming. But how can you ever ready yourself for such an arrival? Twenty-two years…
>
> I need to call Mama from the cooking room, but my feet won't move.
>
> "Are you fine?" I ask.

"I am very well, how are you?"

"I am doing fine too, thank you. Shall I take your bags?" I need to have a moment to collect my thoughts. A small group of the children from the compound are gathering around her, amazed; she towers over them, tall and statuesque. I can see her smiling at the attention, trying to be gracious. She's swept up in it all. The excitement of being here... but it's not real. "Mama, she is here," I call as I bring the bags into the house. I know this is all I need to say.

Mama holds onto the wall near her, as if afraid her feet may fail her. Then she stretches her arms to the heavens: "Oh God!" she shouts in thanks. "You go fetch my kitenge," she says urgently, still with arms stretched to the heavens. More words come out of her mouth, but it sounds like speaking in tongues to me. Between her and her God, I assume.

As I walk out, I see her hurriedly wiping the sweat from her face. Sweat mixed with the tears pouring from her eyes. She staggers a little, as though she doesn't want to move towards Nyakale, but this is all her feet want to do.

"Nyakale Nyakale Nyakale!" she screams, tears streaming down her face. She comes forward slowly at first, but then breaks and throws her entire body at me – like she's been rehearsing for this moment, but her body's decided to act the way it feels anyway. She hugs me tightly, but my arms remain at my sides, lifeless. I feel her modest frame against me. I can smell coal, and the savoury food she was preparing. My mind is blank.

"Oh Nyakale, oh..." Like my name is a prayer.

She steps away from me and studies my face. I look at her and see a bit of me, maybe. She's still crying as she pulls me back into her embrace.

"I am sorry my daughter, forgive me." She spits these words out between sobs.

Before I can answer, she falls to her knees. Now embracing my feet. I can see Achen watching in the distance.

"Please stand up," I whisper.

She doesn't seem to have heard me, so I reach out and help her to her feet. She puts her hand on my shoulder, and we make our way towards the house.

> My mother falling at her feet like that. Is this moment the answer to years of anguish? Nyakale looks like a fish out of water. She's just standing there, not saying a word while our mother pleads with her. What kind of manners are these?

I wake up at five in the morning, in Achen's bed. The plastic is still on the wooden frame and the white bedding smells new. Achen is sleeping on a mattress on the floor. I can't help but feel guilty. Everyone insisted that I take the bed, even Achen, although she looked irritated. My mother sleeps on a mat, and red and orange kitenges are hung to separate the different sections of the house. Now I can hear her and the other women chattering outside, preparing a meal. Pots beating against each other.

Achen gets up. I want to ask her where she's going, if I should go too, but I'm scared to say anything; she doesn't seem to like me.

> Mama is preparing the millet porridge. I can tell she's in good spirits by the way her body is rhythmically swaying. Smiling, exclaiming now and again to anyone willing to hear, "Look what God has done, my daughter has returned!"
>
> I really don't understand the fuss everyone's making. What happened to "When in Rome, do as the Romans"? Why can't she adapt, isn't this the very thing that she left her familiar home for?

This is my home. The industrious mothers awake at dawn, babies on their backs as their hands navigate pots and pans, and their eyes forever watching, seeing that the children stay out of trouble. The fathers who show their love by waking up at five, going out into the world to seek some return from this soil. Taxis and people commuting, navigating, bending and stretching from the moment they wake until the sun hides and the evening drags heavy bodies homeward. All things selfless.

I'm not sure how I feel about her being here. It would be childish, to not want to share my mother's affection. It's just that she gets to miss the years of mourning, and only experience the harvest of Mama's joy. That can't be fair. And I don't like that she thinks she understands this community, because she doesn't. Living is understanding.

I worry about her; that she will not find what she is looking for here.

Over the next days, we go around the villages, house to house: Mama explaining the return of her daughter, and me smiling, the object of fascination on parade. These faces are meant to be known to me, I think repeatedly as we pass through the different compounds. They would be familiar, if not for circumstances, distance and time. "Hi," I say, over and over, wishing there were more words to make this moment easier. But a mind can't retrieve memories that don't exist. I sit watching, smiling, silent.

Even when visiting homes of people who seem worse off than my new-found family, they insist on giving Mama a chicken for me; I marvelled at the finest dishes and drinking mugs set aside for me. This is what dignity looks like: being generous in whatever ways you can.

"Nyakale!" Returning home this evening, I heard someone calling my name – but they were addressing another Nyakale, not me. Here in Uganda I am strange, because of the way I speak, my accent. In South Africa I was different because of my immaculately polished skin, and my name. But my name is a known thing here. It is free. And I am too: uncertain, but certainly free.

I excuse myself to the bedroom, saying I'm tired. I check my phone, wanting to talk to someone, anyone... but there's so much about the last few days that I can't put into words.

Where is Achen? I've seen her walk away from the village several times now, heading for the mountain, but she hasn't yet asked if I want to come with her.

Quietly, I let myself out the back. Evening is falling. Nagoya Mountain rises just outside the village. It's not too far away.

> Here I am again, where I played with Yokolam when we were kids. I close my eyes, trying to still my thoughts, my entire being. I'm exhausted from this, the week the city returned – but not just the city. The past. The mirror image.
>
> The city is delicate and therefore deserves the finest of all things. The city must continuously be asked, "Are you okay?", "Do you want something to eat or drink?", "Tell us stories about South Africa?" The city takes centre stage and the limelight as we stand in the shadows, mute. I expect this from the children – their curiosity draws them easily to things unknown. But I'm surprised by Mama and the elders, bustling like worker bees because the city must get the best of all things. The leftovers for those of us who stayed behind.
>
> The other night, Mama came into our room, thinking Nyakale and I were asleep. I observed her through slitted eyes. She sat in the corner for an hour, watching over us, smiling from time to time. I knew: Nyakale had finally come back home, and that meant Mama had, too.

I'm startled by a sound, like a sob. It's coming from behind a nearby rock. I walk slowly towards it, step by step, and peer over the rock.

Her knees are pulled towards her body, her face buried between her knees.

"Nyakale?" I touch her shoulder gently.

She looks up, eyes red. "Achen."

Slowly, I sit down next to her. My arm naturally finds its place around her back, my hand on her shoulder. Her head rests on my shoulder, her body slightly trembling.

"Please don't cry, Nyakale. Shhhhh…"

And I feel her exhaling, deeply – as if she's been holding her breath for years.

It just makes me want to cry even more. I think of all the moments in my life where having Achen by my side would've made all the difference.

"I have no idea what I'm doing here," I sob. "Why I came. I don't belong here. What am I going to do in Kampala?"

"Well … what if you're not meant to know, but instead find out day by day?" She seems so calm. "Decision by decision. What if that's the lesson?"

"I want to believe you, but I don't know anymore. Your mother, you – I've only known you for a couple of days… I don't really know you at all. Your hopes, what you're afraid of… I know nothing."

"Okay. So ask me something?"

I sniff back my tears, thinking about it. "Like… what was your biggest fear, age ten?"

She is silent for a long moment. "My biggest fear at ten was that our mother would not survive losing you."

I look at her and I see myself; a different self. I wish I could've known. I wish I could do something about it now: retrieve time, change things.

"One day at a time, Nyakale. It all can't happen suddenly.

Little by little, and eventually a lot." She stands up, suddenly smiling, her whole face relaxing. "Come, let me show you something. It's a thing I've done since I was a child on days the world refused to bend in my favour."

She walks towards the edge, where the mountain drops away, and stands there, letting the breeze blow against her. Her eyes are closed; she lifts her arms like they are big, grand wings, gently gliding on the wind.

I have to laugh. I stand up and join her, knowing instantly what she means.

> Standing side by side, I wonder if one day we'll be friends. I know it will take effort, and time. There's so much I want to tell her. About my work, about Yokolam. Does she have stories too? Who will be the first to say something – something real?
>
> Far below us I see the village in the moonlight: children running around, people walking up and down. The weight of the world feels lighter. Maybe there's something bigger than the both of us, a silent master of ceremonies, putting the pieces of the broken mirror back together. Maybe this is part of why I felt so compelled not to leave the village. Somehow I knew I had to be here, for when my sister returned.

Home. Those four letters have always created anxiety in me – the all-explaining, all-encompassing connectedness that they're meant to evoke. But now the realisation settles on me, in all its weight: I am here to stay.

I look up, and the sky is decorated with clusters of stars, like this is where God stores all the extras. I stretch my arms out beside her, like a bird, like a reflection. My heart beating like it still wants to run away, but my feet firmly planted. I am home.

ACKNOWLEDGEMENTS

I'm still overwhelmed by how this story has evolved into something beyond my wildest dreams.

I see a thousand fingerprints on the surface of who I am. If I were to mention everyone who has contributed to me being able to dream wildly, I would need to write a second novel.

To my friends: I value you. It is tremendously humbling to see the world through your eyes and do life with you; to laugh, dream, cry and hope.

To my mother and father: your love has always known no boundaries. Thank you for being the best people I know.

To my siblings and nephew, Ken, Ronny, Jeff, Jackie and JB: for growing up with you and growing old together. Your support gives me wings.

To Sihle Nontshokweni: for sitting with me every Tuesday and Thursday for a month, reading each chapter and giving me honest feedback. Are you even human? Your celebration of my work like it was your own has put so much courage in me.

Sandisiwe Yengeni and Shani du Plessis: thank you for reading the entire manuscript and sending me insightful thoughts and comments. It made the journey of living in this world in my mind a lot less lonely.

To Titi Kabi: for sparking ideas and fleshing out concepts with me. Thanks for lending me your creative flare. Staring at the typewriter you bought me encouraged me on tough days.

Thank you to Busi Kabane for sitting and reliving the Rhodes Must Fall movement with me.

Last but not least, Henrietta Rose-Innes, my editor, for taking my words and delicately making them bloom. To Thabiso Mahlape for believing that together we can make magic.